Bitter Roots

Bitter Roots

A Bitter Root Mystery

C.J. Carmichael

TULE
PUBLISHING

Author's Acknowledgments

I hope my readers enjoy reading Bitter Roots as much as I enjoyed the adventure of writing it. Thanks so much to the team of people who smoothed the way, especially Jane Porter, my dear friend and publisher extraordinaire, and Meghan Farrell, Lindsey Stover and Michelle Morris from the fun and fabulous Tule Publishing company.

I'm so grateful to the team of editors who helped refine and polish the story: Linda Style, Helena Newton and Marlene Engel. Thanks to Frauke Spanuth of Croco Designs for my evocative book cover, and much gratitude also to Lee Hyat and Sharlene Moore who help me with all manner of promotional matters. The fabulous team at Wax Creative, headed by Emily Cotler, manages my website and newsletter distributions-I would not want to be in this business without all of you beside me!

I also want to thank my beta readers Michael Fitzpatrick, Susan Luciuk, Gloria Fournier, and Leslie Archibald. You go first to smooth the way of those who follow!

Chapter One

ZAK WALLER, DISPATCHER for the Lost Trail, Montana, Sheriff's Office, expected the morning after Halloween to be busy, but he hadn't anticipated a homicide case. The call came in early morning just after he'd made coffee.

As was often the case, he'd been the first into the office, and was still the only one here. The sheriff wasn't what you'd call a morning person and Deputy Butterfield, who was nearing sixty, never saw the point in working if his boss wasn't around to notice.

Usually Deputy Black was punctual, but she'd only been on the job about three months so there was still time for bad habits to develop. A former barrel racer, she'd brought her drive and competitiveness into this new career with her. Though she obviously thought she was hot stuff—she was tall, long-limbed, in great shape, and in possession of a confident smile—Zak himself hadn't quite figured out what to make of her.

Earlier Zak had checked the messages and recorded two complaints of Halloween-style vandalism. A report of some flattened pumpkins on the front porch of the library, and, as happened every year, an egged front window for retired schoolteacher Miss Christensen. Both would have to wait.

"Can you slow down and repeat that please?" Zak said to the freaked-out nurse on the other end of the line.

"There's a dead woman on the walkway." Her voice was a little calmer this time. "I found her on my way to work. She's been beaten. Badly. Poor, poor thing." She gave a quiet sob before adding, "Probably been dead for hours. She's so cold…but rigor hasn't set in, so…"

Zak made notes, grateful it was a nurse who had made the discovery, though this one seemed on the verge of losing her professional calm. From his training at the academy—which he'd finally convinced the sheriff to pay for after two years of working and learning on the job with precious little in the way of instruction—Zak knew lots of people blanked out, or panicked in a tragedy. In the simulated emergency situations during his training he'd scored well for his ability to focus logically on what needed to be done.

That same urgent yet calm focus came over him now.

"Don't touch her more than medically necessary. Be careful not to contaminate the scene. Can you give me your name and number please?"

The nurse did so quickly. "You need to send someone right away. It—she looks awful. It's not right that she's just lying out here. Can I cover her up at least?"

"Don't touch anything. I'll have someone there soon." He entered the location, the medi-clinic on Tumbleweed

Road, into his logbook. "You say you're in the rear parking lot?"

"Y-yes. Her—the body—was pushed up against the back entrance."

"Do you recognize her, Farrah?" In a county of less than three thousand citizens, this was more than possible.

"No, but she's young. Early twenties. It's hard to be sure though because…her face is pretty bad."

"I'm going to hang up now to call this in. Stay calm, help will be there soon." He heard voices in the background, someone shouting, *What happened?* "Keep any passersby well back from the scene. Can you do that, Farrah?"

"O-okay."

He called the sheriff first, catching him on his way to the office. "Farrah Saddler, the nurse at the medi-clinic on Tumbleweed, found a woman's body on the street when she showed up for work this morning. Said it looks like the woman's been beaten to death."

"What the hell?"

Zak forgave him his confusion. In all his career Sheriff Ford had probably fielded only a handful of calls like this one. Yes, death occurred here. Lots of it. But potential homicide? Very rarely.

Zak repeated everything Farrah Saddler had told him.

"Okay. I'm only a few minutes away from the scene. Send Butterfield out here. Hell, might as well send Black too. You said the woman looked beaten? Make sure Black has the evidence kit. Oh, and don't forget to call Doc Pittman."

Doctor Pittman was the local coroner and Zak had his number next on the list. He caught the doctor, a widower in his mid to late fifties, at his breakfast table. Pittman took the call with the measured calm of a man who had weathered a good many emergencies in his decades of being the only doctor in town. Pittman assured Zak he'd be at the scene pronto.

"Thanks, Doc." Next Zak called Butterfield, who claimed to be on his way to work, even though Zak could hear his wife talking in the background.

Just as Zak was about to move on to Deputy Black, she stepped into the office. Zak had scored top marks in his anti-bias training, too, but he could not help appreciating the snug fit of her regulation trousers and shirt. She had her golden hair up in a bun, which formed a handy backstop for her aviator sunglasses.

"What are you staring at?" She slung her jacket on a peg, then moved toward the coffee machine.

The woman had attitude, no doubt about it.

"Don't bother pouring that coffee, Deputy. We just had a call—"

"Damn, I hate Halloween. But I'm sure the outraged citizen who had their car egged, or their window broken can wait until I get some caffeine into my system."

"This wasn't about vandalism. We have a suspected

homicide."

She froze, cup only half-full, then set down the pot. "Homicide."

He glanced down at his logbook. "Call came in at seven-fifty. A nurse found a body behind the medi-clinic on Tumbleweed. The woman was dead, her body already cold. The nurse said she'd been beaten." Zak paused before adding, "The sheriff wants you to bring the evidence kit."

"Homicide," Deputy Black said again. Then she smiled. "And I didn't think there'd be any action in this one-horse town." She poured a generous splash of milk into her cup, then downed the coffee in several swallows. When she set down the empty mug she clucked at him with mock sympathy.

"Poor Zak. You have to stay here and mind the phones while we have all the fun."

Zak shrugged. Black often tried to goad him, but as the runt of a litter of four boys—the three oldest much taller and broader than him—he'd learned to never rise to tossed bait.

Black's expression shifted from smug to puzzled. "I don't get it. If you'd applied for the deputy position when Redford retired, you would have been a shoo-in. Not that I'm complaining, since I'd be out of luck if you had. But why the hell didn't you go for it?"

Zak hated having to state the obvious, but Black obviously wasn't going to let this go. "I didn't want the job."

"You actually *like* being a lowly dispatcher?"

Zak's answering smile might be a front, but no way was he going to let on his true feelings about his profession, certainly not to Black of all people.

"What's wrong with you? You're reasonably smart. Not in terrible shape. If you made an effort, in ten years you could probably be sheriff."

"If I don't want to be a deputy, what makes you think I want to be sheriff?"

She stared at him. Curled her upper lip. "You don't make sense."

"Great. I love being an enigma."

Finally he'd shut her up. She snatched the evidence kit and her jacket and left.

Chapter Two

WHEN SEATED AT his law office desk on the second floor of a modest brick building on Tumbleweed Road, Justin Pittman had a clear view of the single-story building across the street that housed both the local medi-clinic and the town's one small pharmacy. So he couldn't help but notice when the sheriff's black SUV pulled up, and the man himself jumped out to the street with significantly more energy than usual.

Sheriff Ford wasn't one for wasted effort, something had to be going on. Justin's hunch was confirmed when Deputy Butterfield showed up a few minutes later, followed shortly afterward by the town's newest deputy. He hadn't met her yet, but his father had approved the hire, stating Nadine Black was exactly what this town needed.

A former rodeo competitor, Nadine was attractive, in her early thirties…and single, Justin's father had made a point of emphasizing.

Of course this had been before Willow showed up in town, with her daughter in tow.

Justin pulled the cord on the window blinds, raising

them to the highest level. It wasn't often the full force of the law in Lost Trail congregated in one place, unless it was after hours for beer and burgers at the Dew Drop Inn. What the hell was going on out there? Sheriff Ford and Deputy Butterfield had moved to the back of the clinic, out of sight. A small group of onlookers was quickly assembling, and soon the new female deputy was waving people out of the way and yellow-taping around the back of the clinic.

And then a very familiar sedan appeared—his father's silver Volvo. Justin's dad emerged from the driver's seat carrying the black case he always took when he was acting in his capacity as local coroner. Someone had died.

Justin checked his watch. His first appointment wasn't for an hour, which left him plenty of time to indulge his curiosity. He left his office and walked through the empty reception room. His hopes of eventually hiring a reception-ist/assistant dimmed with each year that passed since he'd hung up his shingle in Lost Trail. There was hardly enough business in this county to support him—now his wife and child, too—let alone a second employee.

A few times he'd almost offered the position to Willow, who was having a difficult time adjusting to her new role as stay-at-home mom. But she would hate the mundane clerical work, and he suspected she wouldn't be very good at it either.

Willow thrived on excitement, travel, action. Life in Lost Trail, Montana, had held little appeal to her when she'd been growing up and it held even less now. But she had a daughter to think of and he had his father.

So for now Lost Trail would have to do for all of them.

Justin hurried down the stairs to the ground level. On the main floor landing the office door to Dr. Edmond's suite was closed, but Justin could still hear the soft grinding of the dentist's drill and smell the distinctive antiseptic odor.

He pushed through the door to the street and winced as the frosty air on this first day of November hit his face. Justin buttoned his sports jacket as he walked across the street. His father had joined the sheriff and Deputy Butterfield well beyond the taped barrier. Justin eased his way through the onlookers, until he came face-to-face with the new deputy.

"Hi, I'm Justin, Dr. Pittman's son."

She didn't look impressed.

"I work across the street." He nodded to the window front with his name embossed in gold letters, *Justin Pittman P.C. Attorney at Law.*

Still not impressed.

"You need to keep back, sir. We have an investigation going on."

"Someone's died, have they?" He caught a glimpse of his father and tried to catch his eye. But his father was focused on something—or someone—just out of Justin's field of view.

At the deputy's impassive shrug, Justin felt a snap of annoyance. Butterfield or Ford would have given him the inside scoop right away.

"It's not my place to say. I suggest you go back to your office. We won't be releasing details for a while yet."

The deputy moved on, pushing the crowd back from the taped-off area. Gertie Humphrey, who worked at the gas station convenience store, patted his arm.

"They say it's a young woman. Beaten to death."

Justin's heart stalled irrationally before he reminded himself that he'd left Willow, sipping coffee at the breakfast table, only thirty minutes earlier. "Does anyone know who she is?"

"No one's positive, but Cody—who works at Lolo's— figures it might be that new laborer they hired at the Raven Christmas Tree Farm. Riley's her first name, not sure about the last."

"And she'd been beaten?"

"Cody got there before the tape went up. He said her face was all swollen and caked with blood." Gertie shivered. "Who would do such a thing?"

A blast of wind scattered some dead cottonwood leaves across the sidewalk. Gertie tugged her toque firmly over her wiry gray hair, and then moved on, no doubt to share her juicy tidbits with more of the fine citizens of Lost Trail.

Justin gave one last glance at the scene beyond the police tape. He felt badly for his father, having to deal with such an ugly situation. In many respects Lost Trail, Montana, was a model American ranching town. Friendly neighbors, well-kept properties, a charming main street designed to attract tourists from the neighboring ski hill.

But Justin knew—both professionally and personally—about Lost Trail's darker side. No doubt his father had treated many female patients who'd suffered a beating—often at the hand of a violent man who claimed to love her. But to Justin's knowledge, this was the first time one of them had died.

THE DRAMA OF the day was exhilarating but Zak never forgot for a moment that the cause was the violent death of a young woman. He hadn't known Riley Concurran personally—apparently she was relatively new to Lost Trail—but he still felt badly. According to her California driver's license she was only twenty-two. Missed calls on the cell phone that had been found in her back pocket had been traced to Kenny Bombard, the new manager at the Raven Christmas Tree Farm. He'd hired Riley as a temporary employee about a month ago.

Zak had only a moment to wonder what his school friend Tiff Masterson, who now lived in Seattle, would make of this—more death on her family's farm, though this time at least, not someone she loved—before the sheriff called to ask him to track down Riley's next of kin.

"Her cell phone is one of those cheap, prepaid models. Only has a few numbers: her boss and Lolo's Pizza. So that's no use. You'll have to follow up on the address from her driver's license. Got a pen?"

"Sure do, Sheriff." He jotted down the address, then added quickly before the sheriff disconnected, "Um…do you know the cause of death yet?"

"She'd taken a couple hard blows to the head. Doc says she would have lost consciousness immediately and probably died a short time after. He also suspects she was moved during that period. But his preliminary report won't be ready until later tomorrow."

Finding next of kin proved harder than expected. The address on Riley Concurran's driver's license turned out to belong to an old school friend, Emily Blake, who hadn't seen Riley in over four years.

All the young woman could tell Zak was that Riley's father had never been part of her life and that her mother had died five years ago, four months before Riley's eighteenth birthday. There were no other living relatives as far as Emily knew.

"My parents let Riley live with us for a year after her mom died. It was supposed to be only for four months, until she turned eighteen, but Riley was super helpful with housecleaning and stuff, and so Mom let her stay longer."

"When did she move out?"

"About halfway through our first year of college. We

both qualified for state scholarships, but Riley met this guy who really messed with her head. She was super cute, but shy. She hadn't dated much before she met Connor. I never understood what she saw in him. He was a mean dude."

"Do you know his last name?"

"Riley must have told me, but I don't remember. Connor was into drugs and drinking, stuff Riley hadn't been interested in before. Soon she was going to classes stoned and staying out all night with Connor. My parents saw what was happening. We were all worried about her. But when Mom and Dad tried to set some strict rules, Riley moved out."

"Did she stay in college?"

"No. Her boyfriend wanted her to work, so she got a job waitressing at a real dive. I pretty much lost track of her then." Emily paused, then added softly, "I should have made more of an effort. She was a good person, she really was."

"Did you and your parents know she was still using your home as her permanent address?"

"I'm not surprised. We still get mail addressed to her sometimes. Mostly junk from the college. My mom has kept it all somewhere."

Zak made a note to follow up. "Do you remember the name of the bar where she worked?"

"Yeah, Jack's Cellar. I drive past it every now and then and it always makes me think of Riley. I can't believe she's dead…"

Minutes after the call with Emily ended, Zak was still

taking notes. They needed to reach out to the sheriff's office in San Francisco. Get them to make inquiries at the bar and with the Blakes. This Connor fellow seemed like a promising lead, but without a surname locating him could be tough.

A ping from his computer alerted him to an email from Deputy Black, subject line: Crime Scene Photos.

The reality of what had happened truly sank in when he opened the attached images of the victim and the crime scene earlier that morning. Studying them grimly, Zak had flashbacks from his own past. Usually his dad landed his punches where people outside the family wouldn't see them. But one time he'd given Mom a hell of a bruise on the side of her face.

Zak, himself, had rarely been the victim. At a young age he'd mastered the talent of slinking out of a room, or being quiet and unobtrusive when no exit was possible.

What he was looking at here though, exceeded by far anything that had happened in the Waller household. The left side of Riley's face was so swollen and discolored she looked nothing like the photo in the driver's license.

Whoever had done this had been enraged. But what could Riley have done to engender such feelings? She'd been in Lost Trail for barely a month. Surely that wasn't long enough to make this sort of an enemy?

Around noon Butterfield came in with bagged evidence from the scene. His chest was puffed up with self-importance as he dropped the sealed plastic bags containing bits of trash, the victim's phone and wallet, and an empty beer can onto Zak's desk.

"Label these will ya? And get them off to the lab ASAP."

Technically this was Butterfield's job but there was nothing the paunchy lawman enjoyed more than barking orders to those he considered beneath him. And in this office that meant Zak.

Zak honestly didn't mind though. It amused him when people assumed his job as dispatcher was boring. While the sheriff and his deputies might have the more active roles in gathering evidence and interviewing witnesses, he, as the communication hub for the office, ended up with the best overall picture of the investigation.

Since he did all the filing, there wasn't a report in this office that didn't wind up on his desk. He might have the mundane task of sending out the evidence to the crime lab in Missoula, but he was also the first person to find out lab results when they came in.

Between all that and fielding calls, relaying messages, and listening to whatever conversations took place around him, there wasn't much that went on here he didn't know about.

"Is this all of it?" he asked when he was finished with the last label.

Butterfield didn't lift his head from the report he was scratching out. "She had car keys in her pocket, but Black took those. She's out trying to find the car."

"What model of vehicle did she drive?"

"Why should you care?"

Zak shrugged.

After a few seconds Butterfield said, "It's a Ford."

A cog turned over in Zak's mind and he realized that he had, in fact, seen the victim before. He'd even spoken to her.

For the past month or so an old blue Focus with California plates had been parked at the trailhead where he went for his morning run. After the first week, he'd approached the woman sleeping in the back, telling her she needed to find a proper campground. She'd assured him the situation was temporary. She'd seemed vulnerable and young and so he'd looked the other way.

He picked up the phone and called Deputy Black. "I hear you're looking for the victim's car?"

"Damn it, yes. I've been over this town twice, with no luck."

"Give the parking lot at the beginning of Tamarack Trail in Lost Creek Park a try."

Silence. And then: "Any particular reason for the suggestion?"

"Just a hunch."

As he disconnected the call he felt a wave of sadness. If he'd reported Riley's illegal camping earlier, would she still be alive?

Chapter Three

A VEHICLE PARKED haphazardly by the Mountain Side Cemetery caught Zak's attention on his drive home from work. It was past seven o'clock and fully dark. Last to leave the office after an incredibly busy day, Zak craved a quiet evening in his cozy basement apartment, binge-watching a few more episodes of the *X-Files* with his cat Watson. He'd discovered the older series recently and was hooked.

But something felt off here.

Zak pulled his truck behind the small, unfamiliar SUV, then killed his lights. Beyond the glow from the streetlamps, the cemetery was unlit so he grabbed a small flashlight from the glove compartment.

Last night pretty much every residential street in town had been swarming with ghosts, goblins, and superheroes, but tonight the sidewalks and roads were quiet, especially on Winding Down Way, where mostly senior citizens lived in the small bungalows that faced the expansive cemetery.

Did the seniors mind looking out their front windows at their most likely next—and final—real estate purchase? Or did they appreciate the proximity to family and friends already gone?

As Zak left his truck he shone the flashlight in a wide arc. Trees—some spruce, some bare-limbed weeping willows—stood guard over the array of grave markers and tombstones. Zak searched for signs of movement among them but saw none. Next he checked the parked vehicle. No passengers, just a duffel bag and purse in the front passenger seat and a large suitcase in the open cargo area.

An out-of-town guest? If so, why stop here?

He turned and followed the path leading to the graveyard. A keening wind from the Bitterroot Mountains drowned out the sound of his boots on the gravel and dried leaves as he moved up the hill. Over his shoulder he noticed the half-moon momentarily break through the cloud cover, before disappearing again. He walked for almost a minute without seeing anything unusual. Then a silhouette emerged from the shadows: a tall, slim woman—her body encased in a wraparound red wool coat—standing a mere twenty feet in front of him.

He heard her suck in a startled breath, obviously noticing him at the same time. She pulled her hand from the tombstone where it had been resting and took a step away from him.

He was about to identify himself and explain he worked at the sheriff's office, when he recognized her. "Tiff Masterson?"

Her quiet voice was barely audible over the wind. "Is that you, Zak?"

"This is a surprise." He moved closer. "Saw your car and thought some kids might be up to no good."

He hadn't seen Tiff in Lost Trail for years, at least five, maybe more. They'd been childhood friends, going to school together in town from kindergarten until Dewbury Academy had been dissolved and the students parceled out to the bigger regional schools in Hamilton.

Their friendship had survived and grown stronger during those high school years. But they'd drifted apart since she'd left for college.

Seemed like she'd grown taller since her last visit, which wasn't likely. Probably she'd just lost weight. The gauntness in her face emphasized her high cheekbones and her large, wide-set eyes.

"It's good to see you. Your mom must be happy you're visiting." Rosemary Masterson still lived with her older sister Marsha Holmes in the large house on the Raven Christmas Tree Farm, about a mile out of town.

Tiff's gaze shifted sideways. "Not so sure this is only a visit. And Mom doesn't know I'm here, yet."

"Oh?" He glanced at the engraving on the slab of granite she'd been touching. *Casey Masterson, beloved son of Irving and Rosemary.* Tiff's brother had been just twelve years old when he'd died from complications of his congenital heart condition.

Zak didn't need to read the inscription on the adjoining marker. Tiff's father Irving had passed away in a car accident scant months after his son's death. Her mother—also in the car, as well as the aunt—had escaped serious physical injury but had suffered some sort of nervous breakdown and hadn't been the same since.

"Yeah, I know it's weird I stopped here first," Tiff acknowledged.

"They were your family. You'll never forget them. But you're doing well, right? Still enjoying your job at that big CPA firm in Seattle?"

She shifted her gaze. "I was. Now, not so much."

He waited, then finally had to say, "There has to be more to the story."

"I'll tell you sometime over beers at the Dew Drop."

"Let's make it soon." He took a closer look at the older model SUV she was driving. The plates were Bitterroot County, Montana, not a rental.

"Is that a borrowed car?"

"Nope. Mine." She shrugged her narrow shoulders. "Just bought it today."

"So you're here to stay?"

"I suppose."

"Don't sound so excited."

"I didn't mean to put down Lost Trail, Zak. It's just…" She shrugged again. "Coming back is hard. I still feel so angry…"

They'd talked about this lots when they were younger. Tiff blamed the cardiologist for not operating on Casey soon enough. And she blamed her father for his accident, believing he'd taken the easy way out, leaving her and her mother alone to deal with Casey's death.

It seemed the more Tiff's mother retreated into her own little world on the Christmas tree farm, the more Tiff's anger had grown, until finally, moving away had seemed like the smartest—and perhaps only—option for all of them.

As Tiff ran her hand over the grave markers one more time, Zak turned away. "Sorry. I should let you have some privacy."

"That's okay. I was just about to leave anyway." She pushed her hands into the pockets of her coat and ducked her head against the wind. "You're looking very fit—still into running?"

In high school they'd both been into track. "Training for another marathon in the spring." At his last one, in Sacramento, he'd placed in the top ten of his age group. But no one in his life—none of his friends, certainly no one in his family—knew this. "Maybe you can join me on a trail run one day?"

"Not likely. I've been doing some hiking but the running has totally fallen off." She pulled her keys from her pocket, then gave him a closer look.

"So. What else is new, Zak? Mom told me your dad's hardware store closed and you're working at the sheriff's office now."

The liquidation of Waller Hardware had been, in many ways, a positive turning point in his life. Mostly because his parents and three older brothers had decided to blame the citizens of the county for the failure, and leave not just the county but the state of Montana as well.

He alone of the Wallers had opted to stay, to rent a small basement apartment and to find a new job for himself.

"Yup. Been there for over three years now, working dispatch." The position, which was usually filled by a woman and viewed as entry level, suited him well, at least for now.

Lost Trail—now that his family had left—was turning out to be the perfect place for him.

"You answer 9-1-1 calls? I can't imagine there are many of those in a small county like Bitterroot."

"You might be surprised. Besides there's a lot more to the job than that, especially since we have only four of us in the office."

"Is Archie Ford still sheriff?"

"Will be until the day he dies, I guess."

She nodded, then waited a moment before asking, "Do you see much of Derick?"

Back in the day the three of them had hung together all the time. But after Tiff left for college, Derick got wrapped up in his family business, and then he'd fallen in love and married a pretty local girl, a few years younger than them. "Derick's always busy. He's practically running Sparks

Construction since his dad had his heart attack last year. And just two months ago he and Aubrey adopted a baby boy. So he's a father now, too."

"Yeah, I chat with him sometimes on Facebook." She made a face at him, probably her way of giving him grief for not having a profile of his own.

Zak didn't have anything against Facebook per se. He just valued his privacy.

Tiff's gaze shifted to the nearest house on the other side of the cemetery. The pristine bungalow had a tidy yard, fresh paint on the siding, and a pretty autumnal-themed wreath on the front door. And an egg-smeared window.

"Oh no. Looks like Miss Christensen was the target of a Halloween egging."

Damn, he'd forgotten to pass along those vandalism calls today. "Local kids hit her house every year."

"I don't get it. She was such a great teacher and anyway, she's been retired for over a decade."

During her years as a teacher and then principal of Dewbury Academy, Cora Christensen had chosen her favorite students. While Tiff had been one of them, Zak never had, and he understood why kids still targeted her house. Miss Christensen was sweet and caring on the outside, manipulative and mean on the inside. She had a talent for discovering and probing her students' insecurities. She'd certainly homed in on his. But he knew he'd never convince Tiff of that.

"You headed home now?" He shone his flashlight on the

curb so Tiff could safely make it to the driver's side of her car.

"I guess. How about you? Do you still live in the same house?"

"No, that was sold." And good riddance. "I rent a basement apartment from Mr. Gruber, at the far end of this road." He hesitated. "One piece of bad news I should probably fill you in on. A woman was killed sometime last night, possibly early morning. I understand she worked at Raven Farm."

"What?" Tiff's eyes widened as she swung back to face him. "I don't understand. Who was this woman and what happened to her?"

"Her name was Riley Concurran. She moved to town about a month ago and started working at your family's place at about the same time. Last night someone gave her a couple of hard hits to the head and she died. Her body was discovered outside the medi-clinic this morning."

"That's dreadful." Tiff shook her head, as if she could somehow negate the news. "Ed—he's the manager—generally hires two or three employees every fall to help harvest the trees for the season. This year Riley must have been one of them. Poor woman. Do you know who did it?"

"Not a clue so far," he admitted. "Sorry to spring this on your first night home."

"I appreciate the heads-up. I'm sure Mom and Aunt Marsha are going to be beside themselves."

"I wouldn't be surprised."

Tiff opened her car door, then looked back at him. "After my dad died I began to believe there was a dark cloud hanging over Raven Farm. I guess it's still there."

Chapter Four

DESPITE BEING ALLOWED to eat several sweet treats from her Halloween stash after dinner, four-year-old Geneva Pittman was asleep minutes after Justin tucked the quilt up to her sweet, pointed chin.

He sat on the side of her bed, his hand resting lightly on the side of her face. Emotions most fathers would have had years to process were flooding over him, bringing him to the point of tears.

This sweet girl was now his daughter. The official papers had arrived today.

"You're happy?"

Willow—his wife, something else to get used to—was in the doorway. As always it was difficult to read the expression on her lovely face. When he was nineteen her father had backpacked around the world before returning to run the family ranch and he'd brought with him a bride from the Philippines. From her mother Willow had inherited beautiful café latte skin, smooth features, and a small but full-lipped mouth. Her parents were dead now after a terrible fire that had left Willow, in college at the time, with nothing but what she had in her dorm room.

He considered her question. Was she worried he might regret his decision? Or stating a fact that seemed obvious to her?

"Very happy." He went to her, wrapping his arms around her slender waist. She was delicately built and with his height and broad shoulders he worried he must seem threatening. To compensate he tried to be especially gentle when he touched her.

He was about to ask if she was happy, too, but she slipped out of his embrace at the exact moment he had the thought, and headed for the kitchen.

She was on the step stool, reaching into the liquor cabinet over the fridge. "That documentary you wanted to watch is starting in ten minutes. I was going to pour a brandy. Would you like one too?"

"Sure." After receiving the all-clear from his oncologist in July he'd been allowing himself one, sometimes two drinks a night. Willow hadn't been back in his life when he was undergoing chemo, and he hadn't told her about the underlying disease for fear of scaring her away. He felt some guilt about this, but he pushed it aside just the way he'd trained himself to push away fears the cancer might come back.

He waited while she poured the drinks, then put the bottle back into the cabinet.

"Go ahead," Willow told him. "I'll join you in a minute."

He sat in the living room, in his favorite leather chair, and reached for the document he'd set on the side table earlier. There it was in black and white. Crazy how reassured he felt reading those words again as if he, an attorney, could have misunderstood the intent the first dozen or so times.

Ten minutes later Willow joined him, curling her lithe body into the chair next to him.

His gaze went from her impenetrable dark eyes that had always reminded him of hazelnuts, to the gleaming new wedding band on her finger. She wore no other jewelry. She'd always been a minimalist when it came to clothing and accessories.

Did she regret marrying him? Letting him adopt her child?

"You'll be a good father."

Yes. He thought that he would. "I hope to be a good husband as well."

Willow merely smiled.

IT WAS PAST eight when Tiff pulled into the Douglas-fir-lined lane that led to her childhood home. The trees were so stately she felt like she was passing through a tunnel. Happiness, sorrow, anger—all these and more churned inside of her, a complicated stew of emotions that made her stomach ache, and her muscles tense.

She was glad for the unexpected meeting with Zak at the cemetery. Resuming their friendship was one positive about moving home. She'd always appreciated his level-headed, easygoing company. Smarter than he let on, Zak was an underachiever who avoided the spotlight, so she wasn't surprised he was happy settling for a job as a dispatcher, rather than vying for a more demanding position as a deputy.

There were other friends she wanted to renew acquaintance with. Top of the list was Derick, and his wife Aubrey as well. It was Derick, after all, who had convinced her it was time to come home.

The fact that she'd run out of traveling money and had no other place to go had cinched it.

When she emerged at the fork where a hand-painted sign instructed visitors shopping for a Christmas tree to turn left, she went right.

For a moment she lifted her foot from the gas pedal. The sprawling, Montana-styled home where she'd grown up was already decorated for Christmas with green and gold lights along the roof-line and around the pillars of the front porch.

The house promised a certain kind of lifestyle that had died for Tiff along with her brother and father when she was ten years old. The double tragedy should have engendered a special closeness between her and her mother, but the opposite occurred.

After her breakdown, her mom had retreated into a sweet

fog that Tiff could not fathom or penetrate. During the day her mother was either gardening or baking, and if she couldn't do either she slept. A lot. Tiff didn't know if one of her mother's coping mechanisms included drugs, but she suspected it was true, a supposition her aunt, who was a nurse, had more or less confirmed when she'd advised Tiff not to judge her mother too harshly.

"She's suffered a lot. And she didn't have the toughest psyche to begin with."

Tiff didn't know if her own psyche was that tough, either, but she could not continue to live as if the losses hadn't happened. She'd been angry as a child, and she supposed she still was. At the vagaries of DNA that had rendered her perfectly healthy, but her beloved older brother so weak. At the surgeon who hadn't been able to rectify the damage. And mostly at the accident that had stolen her father.

Her aunt insisted a deer on the road had made the outcome inevitable, but this was tough for Tiff to believe. Her father had been on a familiar road in his trusty four-by-four truck with brand-new winter tires.

Even though Tiff didn't believe in curses, she couldn't help feeling her family was under one. Now with an employee having been murdered, it was even easier to believe it. Her years going to college and working at the accounting firm in Seattle had allowed her to put such thoughts out of her mind. But now that she was within sight of this place—her home—she felt the heaviness close in on her again.

She parked her SUV to the right of her aunt's truck. Her mother, who hadn't driven since the accident, had finally sold her own vehicle about the same time as Tiff had left for college.

Other than the Christmas lights, and faint lights in two of the upper-floor bedrooms, the house was dark. She got out of her vehicle and grabbed her overnight duffel bag, pondering what to do.

If there had been lights on the main floor, or in her aunt's room, Tiff would have knocked at the front door. There would have been surprise, then a million questions, and finally an offer of herbal tea and homemade cookies, followed by yet more questions.

But with everyone retired, probably reading quietly in their rooms, it seemed smarter not to create a fuss.

So Tiff headed to the guest cottage, which was always kept clean and stocked with snacks—including, hopefully, a bottle of wine and some beer. By the faint light of the moon, which had just decided to peek out from the clouds again, she followed the path that curved through her mother's perennial flower beds, past the rock garden, and finally the fruit trees.

No sparkling lights adorned the small log cabin or its simple porch. Two cedar chairs flanked the front door, a woolen blanket draped over one invitingly. Picture-perfect. Oddly, Tiff could now smell a wood fire. The odor must be a remnant from earlier that evening. Or perhaps her aunt had left the fire burning when she went to bed, after closing the glass doors to prevent sparks from escaping.

Strange that Spade, the family dog, hadn't barked. Tiff paused a moment to listen but the night was dead quiet.

And then, just as she was reaching for the door handle, she heard three gruff barks.

At the same moment the door swung open and a tall man with dark, wavy hair stared out at her, his muscular body blocking a squirming and panting Spade.

"What the hell—?"

"Who are you?"

Their questions came out at the same time, and were followed by several seconds of silence as they looked each other up and down.

Shadowy flickers of light suggested a wood fire was burning in the otherwise dark room. The dancing flames revealed a man who could have been her age, or five years older. His feet were bare and he was wearing jeans and a plaid shirt. He had a beer in one hand and she could hear a hockey game playing quietly in the background. The man had strong features, a dark scruff of a beard, and deep-set, intense eyes.

"You must be Tiffany," he said in a scratchy baritone.

"Tiff."

"I'm Kenny Bombard. The new farm manager."

Spade finally pushed out from behind the man and pressed his big, soft body against Tiff's legs. She bent to give the old dog a few scratches and a kiss on the head, taking her time so her brain could have a chance to process. Apparently she wasn't the only one in the family who hadn't been sharing her news lately.

"What happened to Ed?"

"He took early retirement."

"Ed was what—mid-forties?" Had to be more to the story than that.

Kenny shrugged. "Ask your aunt for the details."

"And why is Spade out here with you?"

"Ah, he's getting older. Almost deaf and having lots of accidents. I offered to keep him here. No carpets. Easier to clean."

"So you live here?" But why? Surely finding a place to stay in town couldn't be that difficult.

"Since I'm new to the area, your aunt offered. So far it's working okay." He glanced at the duffel bag she was still carrying. "You weren't planning to sleep here, were you?"

Of course she was, and he knew it. "It's late. Didn't want to disturb my mom and aunt."

"You hung the moon where they're concerned. Don't think they'll mind if you wake them."

"No. I suppose not."

He must have picked up on her reluctance, because he opened the door wider. "Unless you'd care to come in for a beer?"

The invitation, from a stranger in her own home, ticked her off. Even more annoying was her temptation to say yes.

"Maybe another time." She backed off with a wave of her hand, and headed back to the main house. Her mom and aunt had a lot of explaining to do.

But then, so did she.

Chapter Five

"M OM?" TIFFANY HAD gone to the glass-paned French doors at the back of the house when she saw the kitchen light flash on. She would have preferred to meet up with her aunt first—Marsha would be less anxious, have fewer questions, and generally be easier to deal with— but it was far more likely her restless, insomniac mother had heard her.

"Tiffany, it *is* you."

Her mother was in her housecoat, looking thinner and much older than the last time Tiff had seen her. Tiffany opened her arms, accepting her mother's tight hug. After several long seconds, her mother reached up to cup her hands on either side of Tiff's face. Her tired eyes, still a striking dark blue, like Tiff's own, studied her intently.

"You're so tanned. But too thin."

"I'm fine." If she'd lost a few pounds during her travels, her mother had lost even more during the two years since Tiff's last, brief visit. "How are you?"

"Fine. Just fine."

"You look tired, Mom."

"Oh, I've had a few bad nights. It was almost two in the morning yesterday when I finally fell asleep. Just a few minutes later I was woken by a sound that I could have sworn was someone driving into the yard. Of course I had to get up and look, but there was no one. Just my imagination, I guess." She gave a disparaging shrug. "But why am I going on like this? Come in, sweetheart. Sit down. I'll get you some cookies and…what would you like to drink? Cocoa…herbal tea?"

"No need to fuss."

"I haven't seen you in two years and you ask me not to fuss. Impossible." As she spoke, Rosemary piled a plate with sugar-dusted gingerbread and chocolate chunk studded oatmeal cookies.

"Who is that man in the guest house?"

Her mother paused. "You've met him already?" Some of the excitement dimmed from her eyes. "You must have gone to the guest cabin, then."

"I know how hard it is for you to get a good night's sleep. I didn't want to disturb you."

"But I was awake," her mother said softly. "You must have seen the light."

Home for just five minutes and she'd already hurt her mother's feelings. But how could she tell her mom she hadn't been prepared to see her? If only the darn cottage had been empty all would have worked out fine.

"So the man…? He said his name was Kenny Bombard."

"He's been here for about six months. Your aunt hired him after Ed left. He's working out surprisingly well, but I still miss Ed. I'll never forget the way he stepped up when we really needed him."

"After Dad died you mean?"

Her mother's lips trembled as she nodded and set the plate on the table. She preferred euphemisms over plain talk. Tiff knew this, so why was she already pressing buttons that could only add strain to her fragile relationship with her mother?

"Cocoa or herbal tea?"

Her mother's favorite tactic. Paper over a difficult moment with the offer of a hot beverage.

"Water is fine for me."

While her mother filled a glass with ice, Tiff eyed the cookie offerings. She could smell the ginger and chocolate from where she was sitting. No doubt these had been baked fresh today. Though eating a cookie felt like a surrender of some sort, Tiff couldn't resist. Her fingers hovered for a few moments, then finally she went for the ginger.

The first bite was heavenly. Soft and chewy texture, with a seductively sweet, buttery, ginger flavor.

"No one makes cookies the way you do, Mom."

The gratification on her mother's face was almost painful to see. It was as if her entire worth as a human being hinged on her ability to bake well.

"Please sit down so we can talk."

Her mother perched on the edge of a chair. When Tiff pushed the plate toward her, she eyed the cookies but didn't take one.

"So why did Ed leave?" He'd been in his late twenties, with three years' experience working at the farm, when her father died. Tiff didn't know if he'd ever been officially offered the job of manager…he'd just stepped into the role during the weeks when her mom and aunt were recovering from the accident, planning the funeral, and dealing with her dad's death.

At that time her aunt had still lived in her own home, but in the months that followed she'd begun spending so much time helping her sister it seemed silly to keep up two separate residences. Rosemary, who couldn't stand to sleep in the room she'd shared with her husband, had moved to the room over the garage and insisted her sister take the master.

"Ed and his wife moved to…I think it was Philadelphia. Their daughter is married and just had a baby. They wanted to be closer."

"What will Ed do in Philadelphia?" Tiff doubted the skills of running a Christmas tree farm were all that transferable.

"I'm not sure." Noticing some crumbs on the table, Rosemary went to the sink for the dish cloth.

An inability to sit still and carry on a conversation was another thing about her mother that Tiff found annoying.

"So how did this Kenny fellow come into the picture?

Where did you even hear of him?"

"Marsha posted a few ads around town and almost immediately this nice young man gave us a call. He needed a job and a place to live… It was perfect timing."

Almost too perfect. "Did you check his references?"

"I think Marsha must have…"

Oh, Lord. "Why didn't you tell me about this?"

"How could I? You've never been good about phoning home. But lately, I swear it's impossible to reach you."

Tiff waited until her mother finished rinsing the dish rag at the sink. Once the faucet was turned off, the only sound in the room was the humming of the refrigerator. "I've been doing some traveling out of the country. I did send you emails when I had Wi-Fi." Though admittedly none of the emails had said much.

Her mom turned from the sink. "A business trip?"

"I'm not with the firm anymore." Tiff drank some water to steady her nerves. There was no reason to worry her mother with the full story. "I quit in the spring and decided to see a bit of the world. I'm sorry I didn't tell you. I didn't want you to worry."

"You've been traveling for half a year and you didn't tell me because you didn't want me to worry?" Her mother's eyes were filling with tears. "I know we aren't close. But seriously, Tiffany, how could you?"

"You get so stressed when I take a simple business trip to New York or LA… I didn't want you spending sleepless nights worrying about me in South America."

"Is that where you were?" Her mother wrapped her arms around her middle. "If your father was alive, you would have told him. He was always your favorite. I can't blame you. Your father was a wonderful man."

"Mom. Please. Don't do this."

"I know I'm a burden. So silly and useless. All I'm good at is baking cookies…and no one wants cookies anymore. Not unless they're gluten-free and low in sugar. You only had one to be polite…"

Her mother whisked the plate from the table, dumped the cookies into the trash.

"No, they were good. I loved the one I ate. Why are you throwing them away?"

Her mom was sobbing now.

"South America. And I didn't even know."

"I'm sorry. I should have told you."

"What about Craig? Did he go with you?"

Tiff curled her fingers around the glass of water. Should she pretend…?

But her mother figured it out before she could fashion an appropriate white lie.

"Let me guess. You and Craig aren't together anymore."

Tiff sucked in a long breath.

"And of course you didn't tell me. Why would you? If what I thought mattered at all you would have brought him home to meet me. But in all the years the two of you were together, you never bothered."

Tiff lowered her head. Last Christmas she'd planned to bring Craig with her to Lost Trail. Then a client emergency had made it impossible for her to get away at all. Now she regretted putting her job before her family, but back then she'd truly felt she was on track to becoming a partner. "I am sorry about that."

"How did we end up like this, Tiffany? Wasn't I a good mother to you? I think back to when you were a little girl and I wonder what I did wrong, but for the life of me I can't figure it out."

Tiff took a deep breath, willing back her tears. "You were a good mother."

Before her brother and dad died, she'd been the best. And maybe that was what hurt the most, even more than the deaths.

And then the door from the hall swung open and into the fray stepped Aunt Marsha.

"Good heavens." Marsha, with her matronly build and sensible chenille robe, came into the room. She was taller than her sister, with a short, practical haircut and handsome features. Marsha looked from Rosemary to Tiff.

Tiff swabbed at her eyes with her sleeve. "Surprise."

"Indeed. And such a lovely one." Marsha crossed the room and gave her a hug that was warm but undemanding.

"You look beautiful. And you're so tanned. Have you just been on vacation?"

Tiff gave her mom a worried look before recapping the news of her resignation and subsequent travels for her aunt's benefit.

Marsha took it in stride. "My goodness a lot has changed for you. I'm glad you've come home. You probably need some peace and quiet for regrouping. And Rosemary—my dear sister, you've gotten all emotional. Let me make you some herbal tea to help you settle."

Within moments the strained atmosphere was gone and the mood in the room became cozy and cheerful. No one mentioned the employee who had died—been killed, according to Zak—and not wanting to unsettle the mood, Tiff didn't either. Marsha brewed Sleepytime tea for all of them, and it seemed to Tiff her aunt added a drop of something special to her mother's.

For the first time all day, Tiff felt the pressure in her neck and shoulders begin to ease. She glanced around the room, looking for changes. There were a few. The walls had been painted a fresh pale yellow, and the dishwasher looked like a new model. But everything else was familiar. The noisy old fridge, the big farm sink. The stainless-steel canister set Mom had inherited from Grandma Holmes. And beside the stove, the ceramic hot plate Casey had made in school for Mother's Day.

This kitchen was undeniably home.

But why hadn't she noticed any of this, felt any of this, earlier?

Why was everything that came so easily when she was around her aunt such a struggle when it was just her and her mom?

Chapter Six

WEDNESDAY MORNING TIFF was awake in time to watch the sunrise from her bedroom window. It had been a rough night. During her travels she'd slept surprisingly well, but her homecoming must have triggered something in her subconscious because the bad dreams were back.

She'd opened a window last night and so her room was cold. She lingered under the warm covers, alternately admiring the morning sky and studying her immediate surroundings. The walls were still painted a pale pink and decorated with unframed calendar pictures of puppies and horses—her earliest passions.

Nothing in the room suggested that the ten-year-old girl who had decorated the room had ever grown up. No posters of her favorite bands as a teenager, no stacks of the fashion magazines she'd devoured trying to learn how to apply makeup and dress like an adult. Even the novels on the bookshelves reflected her younger favorites including the entire Heartland series by Lauren Brooke. Where were all the books she'd read during high school?

It was as if she and her mother had conspired to curate

this home as a testament to the days when Casey and her dad had been alive, back when there had still been horses on the property, and her mother's laughter in the kitchen.

Mother.

Guilt weighed down on her, heavier than any down-filled quilt. How had she managed to bring her mom to tears so quickly…on her first night home, no less? Tiff felt two equal and opposite impulses. One was to get in her car, drive far away, and never look back.

The other was to try and make a fresh start. To be kind to her mother. And patient.

She could manage that—couldn't she?

It was a worthwhile resolution to start the day.

After a quick shower and change of clothes, Tiff went down to the kitchen, where her mood was instantly light-ened at the sight of sunlight streaming in the south-facing windows and her aunt Marsha at the table with a cup of coffee and the morning paper. Shame followed quickly on the heels of her pleasure. She was supposed to *want* to see her mother.

Marsha set down her paper. "Good morning. How did you sleep?"

Such a relief to face a simple, unloaded question. "Not the best. How about you?"

"Oh, I always sleep well. I have my years in nursing col-lege to thank for that. Your mom took a while to settle down, I suspect. She'll probably make up for it by sleeping in a bit."

"Yes." It was Rosemary's usual pattern, up until the wee hours, then in bed until practically noon. Tiff went to the coffee pot and helped herself. "So how have you been, Aunt Marsha? Are you still working at the clinic?"

"Just two days a week now. Dr. Pittman hired a new nurse last year, Farrah Saddler. She's working out quite well."

From her aunt's tone it was impossible to say whether she was pleased about this.

"Do you think you'll ever retire completely?"

"Maybe when I'm sixty. I won't be difficult to replace. Dr. Pittman, though, is another matter. Attracting a replacement doctor to our small town will be close to impossible."

And yet the doctor surely would want to step down soon. He had to be a good five years older than her aunt.

"I guess people will just have to go to Hamilton." The hour-long drive wasn't bad in good weather, but during a blizzard or big rainstorm, it might be a problem.

Tiff brought her coffee to the table. "What can you tell me about the new farm manager? Mom said you checked his references."

Periodic flashbacks of her short conversation with Kenny had punctuated her restless night. Tiff couldn't say why. Was she attracted to him? Or worried about him? She thought a little of both.

"Yes, I certainly did. He's well known in backcountry skiing circles. He used to be a ski guide for those places where you need a helicopter to get to the hills, but he injured his knee about eighteen months ago. It's mostly healed now, but he'll probably never ski professionally again."

"So what drew him here?"

"He was staying with a buddy in Missoula when he saw our ad posted online. He had been looking for an outdoor job, one that wasn't too strenuous. We had him out here for a trial week and he learned the ropes quickly. He also handled the seasonal hires—though that has turned out to be a bit of a problem." Marsha bit the side of her lip.

Tiff guessed where her aunt was heading and stepped in to make it easier for her. "I ran into Zak last night when I stopped in town. He told me one of our employees was killed a few nights ago."

"Yes." Marsha covered her face with her hands as she took a moment to compose herself. Finally she dropped her arms. "It's so awful to think about. Her name was Riley Concurran and she was such a pretty young woman. I thought she looked too delicate for the job but Kenny and Bob assured me she had no trouble keeping up with the rest of the crew."

"What happened exactly?"

"All we know for certain is that her body was found outside the medi-clinic the morning after Halloween. I wasn't working that day so it was poor Farrah who found her. They say she'd been hit brutally on her head but no one seems to have any idea who would do such an awful thing. She'd only been in town about a month."

"How awful."

"Kenny says she wasn't the type of person who made enemies. She was sweet and accommodating, at least according to him."

Kenny. The name reminded Tiff of her annoyance from last night. "The lights were off on the main floor when I arrived last night so I went to the guest cottage first thinking I could sleep there for my first night."

If her move here turned out to be permanent as she suspected it might, she'd hoped to take up long-term residence in the cabin. At thirty she felt a little old to be under the same roof as her mother and aunt. But that plan obviously wasn't going to work.

"I'm sorry, Tiff, but we've lent the cabin out to Kenny."

"So I discovered." An image flashed in her mind. Kenny at the door, in bare feet, his dark eyes looking at her with undisguised interest. She cleared her throat. "Couldn't he rent a house in town like Ed did?"

"I suppose. But the cottage was empty. And I think your mother feels more secure having a man on the property at night."

Tiff contemplated that. She knew her mother had a nervous constitution, but she'd never thought personal security was one of her issues. After all, it had been just the three of them—all females—living here since her brother and father died.

"I wonder—" Before she could finish, a knock sounded on the French door. Through the glass panes Tiff could see Kenny, a cell phone in hand. The man was fully dressed this morning, in jeans, a work shirt and black down vest, and steel-toed boots.

Marsha waved him inside and he wiped his boots on the mat by the door before stepping in.

"Just had a call from the sheriff," he said.

A chill passed over the back of Tiff's neck. She stared into the manager's dark eyes, mesmerized by them and the solemn tone of his voice. After what felt like several long, quiet seconds, Kenny glanced back at her aunt.

"He has some questions about Riley." He turned to Tiff. "Have you heard…?"

"About her death? Yes."

He nodded. "The sheriff wants to talk to all of us—well, not you, Tiff, but your aunt and your mother."

Tiff checked the time. It wasn't yet nine. "Did he say when he'd be here?"

"He wanted to come at ten, but I know Rosemary isn't much of a morning person. I put him off until eleven."

"Well done, Kenny," Marsha said. "I'd better go upstairs and start prepping Rosemary. I'm not sure how she's going to take being interviewed for a murder investigation."

Chapter Seven

TIFF'S MOTHER WAS on her first coffee of the day when Sheriff Ford knocked on the front door to ask his questions. It was Tiff who answered the door, blinking rapidly as the abstract news of an employee's death morphed into the reality of an official investigation.

"Come in, Sheriff. Mom's in the kitchen."

Sheriff Ford hadn't changed much from how she remembered him. A big man, in both height and girth, with a buzz cut and a plump face that would have put her in mind of Santa Claus except the sheriff almost never smiled.

On their way past the central staircase, he paused at the family photo on the wall. Taken the Christmas before Casey died, the four of them were posed by the fireplace, parents standing together at the back, with arms around their children in the front. What a happy, loving group they looked back then.

The sheriff grunted—whether in sympathy, sorrow, or merely as an acknowledgment, it was hard to say.

Rosemary stood as soon as they entered the room. She had dark bags under her eyes and her complexion was wan, but at least Marsha had made sure she was dressed and her hair was brushed and held back by a clip at her nape.

"Good morning, Sheriff. You must be here about that poor, poor girl…" Rosemary paused delicately. "It sounds like a terrible business."

"Yes and I'm sorry to disturb you with it, Rosemary, but I do have some questions." The sheriff glanced around the room. "Is your new manager around? I need to talk to him, as well."

"I'll go get him," Tiff offered, but through the French doors she could see Marsha and Kenny were already heading for the house.

"Would you like some coffee, Sheriff?" Rosemary switched to hostess mode and soon had a plate piled with cookies on the table. Not the gingerbreads and chocolate chip ones from yesterday. These were pretty shortbreads, cut in the shape of snowflakes, with silver frosting accents.

"Yes to the coffee, Rosemary. It's been a long day." His hand hesitated over the cookie plate. "These look too pretty to eat."

"But that's what they're for," Rosemary assured him.

Still feeling guilty about last night, Tiff took a cookie and bit into it. "Beautiful and delicious too, Mom. You've still got the touch."

The back door opened and a gust of cool air followed Marsha and Kenny into the house. Both had red cheeks and were breathing rapidly enough to suggest they'd been hurrying.

"Sheriff Ford," Marsha said. "I saw you drive up and ran to get Kenny."

Noticing there weren't enough chairs at the kitchen table for all of them, Tiff went to grab an extra from the adjoining dining room, but Kenny was a step ahead of her.

His simple, "I've got it. Go ahead and sit down," made her cranky. She didn't like the easy familiarity he seemed to have with her mother, her aunt, this house—hell he even had the family dog literally eating out of his hand.

"Sit down, honey," her aunt said with a smile, and Tiff obliged, watching as Kenny, having positioned the extra chair, went to grab a mug from the cabinet as if hanging out in her family's kitchen was something he did every day.

Ed had been a mild-mannered, soft-spoken man who had showed up every day to work at the barn and almost never came around the main house or the women who lived there. She couldn't remember him ever sitting casually in the kitchen with them, let alone moving the furniture and helping himself to the coffee. Not that she would have minded any of the above. Ed had earned the right to be considered part of the family. Not so Kenny.

"So I need to know the last time you saw Riley," the sheriff said, once they were all seated. "How was she acting and did she give any indication there were problems in her life? We're also having trouble tracking next of kin and I hope you can help us with that too."

"You'll have to answer him, Kenny," Marsha said. "I've seen Riley around the yard a few times but we were never close enough to speak. I suspect it's the same for you, Rosemary?"

"I took some cookies out for the workers on Monday." Rosemary plucked a crumb from the tabletop and placed it in her saucer. "I met the girl—Riley—then. She was so thin. I felt sorry for her. I asked if she was getting enough to eat and she said yes, but I didn't believe her. I gave her an extra bag of cookies to take home."

"How long had Riley Concurran been working here?"

"She replied to the ad I put out early in October," Kenny said. "Started working October fifteenth, along with three other guys, all of whom have worked here before. Riley was the only new hire, and frankly the main reason I took her on was I felt sorry for her. She looked kind of desperate."

"How so?"

"Really skinny, as Rosemary said. From her beaten-up old car, faded jeans, and torn jacket it was pretty clear money was tight." He shrugged. "She could be skittish, too, as if she was used to harsh treatment."

"Did you check references?"

Kenny shifted in his chair. "She didn't have any. Said she'd spent the past few months straightening out her life. She'd come to Lost Trail to get away from some people who had been a bad influence. What she needed was hard work and a fresh start. If I'd give her a chance."

Tiff's annoyance with the man went up a notch. "Did you stop to wonder if my mother and aunt would want someone like that working on our property?"

"Kenny did ask us, honey," Marsha said gently. "We agreed the young woman deserved a break."

"I kept a close eye on her especially the first week. For all that she was small and thin, she worked hard, baling trees and loading them on the trucks just as fast as the guys."

"Did you see any signs of her drinking or using drugs?" the sheriff asked.

"Nope. Never."

"Did she work the full day on Halloween?"

"Yup, regular hours, from eight to five."

"And her mood, was it same as usual?"

"Now that I think of it, she seemed kind of jittery."

"Maybe she had plans to meet someone. Did she ever mention a boyfriend?"

"She never mentioned anyone. I got the impression she kept to herself. I'm pretty sure she was living in her car. It was jammed with stuff. Clothes, books, a sleeping bag. Shortly after she was hired she asked if I'd mind if she used the shower in the barn."

"There's a shower in the barn?"

"Irving's mother insisted on it. Her husband always showered at the end of his work day before he entered the house. I was never so strict with Irving." Rosemary sighed, shifting her gaze to the window that looked out to the big red barn, as if hoping to see her husband one more time.

Tiff sighed too, remembering how she had loved the outdoors piney smell of her dad when he came in for his dinner at the end of the day. Because of his bad heart, her brother had been discouraged from helping with any but the simplest of outside chores, and to be fair to Casey, she hadn't been encouraged to hang out around the barn much either. So dinner was often the first they saw of their early-rising father every day.

The one exception was during the three-week span between Thanksgiving and Christmas. During the holiday season she and her brother were allowed to hang out with the customers in the barn, sometimes helping in the small shop that sold Christmas decorations, or handing out the free apple cider and cookies their mother always provided. The last year he'd been alive, Casey had been in charge of the adding machine and the cash box, a responsibility he'd loved.

"Anyway," Kenny resumed, "I told Riley she could use the shower whenever she wanted, and most days after work she did."

"Do you remember if she showered on that day?"

"Yup." Kenny looked on the verge of saying more, but only swallowed and looked away.

"Can you describe her car?"

"An older model Ford Focus. Blue with Californian plates." Kenny gave the sheriff the license number, reciting it twice when the sheriff mixed up two digits.

"Did you take down her next of kin when you hired her?"

Kenny pulled his phone out of his pocket. "I figured you'd be asking, so I took a photo of the employee record I have for her. It's kind of hard to read on this screen, but she gave a name and address of an Emily Blake from San Francisco."

The sheriff seemed disappointed when he heard that, but he didn't elaborate. "You think these bad influences she was trying to get away from might have tracked her here to Lost Trail?"

"I guess it's possible but we never saw any of them here on the farm."

The sheriff grunted, then got up from the table. "I may have more questions later. This will do for now. While I'm here though, I'd like to talk to the other fellas who worked with Riley."

"The men are out in the field right now. I'll call my foreman, Bob Jenkins, and ask him to bring the crew to the barn ASAP," Kenny said.

Tiff's mother pressed her hands to her chest as if trying to buffer her heart. "You can't think one of our employees did this terrible thing?"

The sheriff softened his tone. "These are routine questions, Rosemary. Sounds like this young lady had a rough past that finally caught up to her. If that's the case, our perp will be long gone by now, don't you worry."

Chapter Eight

A LATE AFTERNOON text message from Zak, inviting Tiff to meet him at the Dew Drop Inn at six-thirty, was a welcome bright spot to her day. She tried reaching out to Derick to see if he and his wife wanted to join them, but it seemed Derick was too busy to go on Facebook today.

Tiff arrived at the pub first and snagged a quiet table in the corner. About a third of the tables were occupied, not bad for a Wednesday night. Above the bar, a football game was playing, sound muted. Only one guy—someone in his forties, cupping his draft in both hands—seemed to be watching.

When the server came, a young woman wearing a Grizz T-shirt, probably one of the owner's daughters—there were three, but Tiff didn't remember their names—she ordered a beer. Then she pulled out her phone. She'd spent the afternoon helping her mother mulch the perennial flower bed in preparation for winter and dirt still clung under her nails, despite the shower she'd taken before dinner.

Tiff had worried her mom would be upset when she learned about Tiff's plans to go out for the evening, but she'd actually seemed relieved. The visit from the sheriff, coupled by hours in the garden, had obviously exhausted her.

A message from Derick pinged into Tiff's Messenger app at the same moment the server delivered a tall glass of draft ale.

"Thanks," Tiff said, barely glancing up from the screen.

"Wish I could," Derick had replied, "but I'm needed at home. Joys of being a new dad."

Tiff read it a second time, more than a little offended.

About four months ago Derick had reached out to her on Facebook. She was two months into her travels, the pain and humiliation over her screw-ups still so fresh she wanted to crawl into a hole and die. Instead she'd hiked the Machu Picchu trail. Later, resting up at a hostel, she'd logged into her Facebook for the first time in ages and that was when she'd seen the messages from Derick.

He'd told her his marriage was in trouble and he didn't know what to do. Aubrey wanted a baby so badly and he'd just found out his low sperm count was the reason they hadn't been able to get pregnant in the five years they'd been married.

He wasn't looking for advice, just someone to vent to. Tiff was only too happy to focus on someone else's problems for a change, diverting any of his questions about her by circling back to him.

When he'd told her he and Aubrey were considering adoption, she'd cheered him on and wished him luck.

The actual adoption itself had come together quickly. After Brody entered his and Aubrey's lives, Derick's mood changed for the better. He shared pictures of the baby and told her how Aubrey was loving being a mother.

"You should come home and meet the new addition," he'd told her. "It's been way too long since you were back in Lost Trail anyway."

She'd been in Puerto Viejo, Costa Rica, worn out from five months of backpacking and spending the last of her money on a hostel near the beach. Coming home had been on her radar, but she would have put it off a little longer if Derick hadn't been so insistent.

And now he was brushing her off?

She felt like she was back in high school where she'd been the class brain and Derick the much more popular football star. Derick had barely acknowledged her existence until his football coach lined her up to tutor him in math, and Zak to help with his language arts. Spending time together in the school library and Derick's home, Tiff had quickly come to understand that Derick was more shy than arrogant.

Soon she, Derick, and Zak were hanging out together just for fun. And the more time she spent with Derick the more she liked him. He never used his imposing size to bully others, or lorded his family's relative prosperity over his classmates, most of whom were children of ranchers, incomes subject to the highs and lows of cattle prices and the vagaries of the mountain weather.

His innate kindness made this brush-off even harder to understand.

"Sorry I'm late," Zak apologized as he pulled out a chair at their table.

She hadn't seen him coming, even though she'd sat facing the entrance. "That's okay. I imagine you've had a busy day." Zak, usually so laid-back he seemed five minutes from sleep, was practically vibrating with energy tonight.

"I'll say. This is the first homicide since I started working at the sheriff's office. I bet it's the first in a decade or more."

"And it happens the very night I move back home after eight years away. I hope I'm not on the suspect list."

She'd meant the comment as a joke but Zak replied with unsettling seriousness. "The way that woman was beaten…I'd say our perp is a man and a strong one."

"Well, the new manager Mom hired certainly fits that bill." She immediately regretted her spiteful comment. "Sorry. Not sure where that came from."

Zak looked thoughtful. "You're talking about Kenny Bombard, right? You don't like him?"

"I don't know him. It's just—he seems to have made himself very much at home on our farm. He's even moved into the guest cottage. Which I had been counting on for myself."

"He was Riley Concurran's boss. What do you think his motive might have been?"

"Stop! I'm sorry. I wasn't seriously putting Kenny forward as a suspect."

"I wonder if they had some sort of personal relationship."

"Cut it out, Zak." She noticed the server and waved her over. "This man needs a beer."

"And a burger with fries. Hold the onions please, Mari."

The busy woman barely nodded, then turned to Tiff. "Anything else for you?"

Her beer was more than half gone. "Sure, I'll have another. Plus a burger and fries too. Lots of onions."

Once the server was gone, Zak folded his arms on the table and leaned forward. "So how was your homecoming? Was your mom excited to see you?"

"I made her cry in the first fifteen minutes. But yeah. She seemed glad I was home."

"Have you etched your departure date in stone yet?"

She rubbed at a circle of condensation on the oak table. "I wasn't kidding when I said I'm considering staying. I might start my own accounting business."

She kept her gaze lowered, but could feel Zak's incredulous stare. Finally he said, "You are aware this is the most sparsely populated county in Montana? Where, exactly, do you hope to find your clients?"

"It'll be a slow build," she agreed.

"Ha! I'll say." Zak leaned back in his chair as Mari came with their drinks and burgers. Zak took a sip of the beer, then lifted the top bun off his burger. "Damn. I thought I smelled onions."

Mari was already gone to the next table. "Want me to flag her down?"

"Nah. I'll scrape them off." He did so with meticulous care, then took his first bite.

"I thought you'd be more excited about me moving home."

"I remember how anxious you were to leave this place. Something bad must have happened to make you want to return."

She turned from him to the wall covered with photos taken from the nearby ski hill. This place did the most business during ski season, which wouldn't start until December and lasted until March or mid-April depending on the snow.

"Things kind of fell apart for me in Seattle."

"Want to talk about it?"

She'd worked hard the last six months to avoid thoughts about the disastrous two months that had preceded her being fired. "Eventually. I might need another beer or two."

"I take it Derick isn't joining us tonight?" Zak took another bite of his burger.

"He's pulling daddy duty." She didn't share her annoyance. Though she was tempted to tell Zak about her and Derick's Facebook exchanges, she decided to wait until she'd had a chance to see Derick in person.

Maybe tomorrow evening she'd drop by their house with

a baby gift. She'd no sooner come up with this plan than she noticed a tall, blonde woman enter the bar. Though wearing a nondescript outfit of jeans and a bomber-style jacket, she had an aura of confidence and strength that naturally drew attention, as Tiff could tell when almost every man swiveled his head to get a better look.

"Who's she?"

Zak, alone of all the men, looked unimpressed. "Nadine Black. Sheriff hired her this year after Greg Redford retired."

"She looks...athletic."

"Used to be a barrel racer. Was pretty good, too. She quit last year when her horse died in the ring at the Pro Rodeo circuit finals in Great Falls."

"That's tough."

Nadine was looking around for a place to sit and her gaze paused when she spotted Zak, who nodded in acknowledgment. Her eyes shifted toward Tiff, and her eyebrows went up.

"Want to invite her to join us?"

"Nah. We see enough of each other at work."

It seemed an odd comment coming from Zak who mostly liked everybody. "You don't get along?"

"We get along fine but she's used to being the center of attention in the rodeo ring. Now she's power-tripping on being a deputy and lording her position over mine. I don't care. I like being a dispatcher."

"That look she just gave you didn't seem condescending

to me. Maybe you're reading her wrong."

"Don't be crazy. I—hang on a second, the local news is coming on."

Everyone in the room—including Nadine Black who had settled on a barstool with her back to them—was now focused on the TV screen. The bartender jacked up the volume.

"*Our top story tonight comes from the small community of Lost Trail, three hours south of Missoula, near the border of Idaho. Sometime late on Halloween night a woman was beaten to death. Her body was discovered the next morning behind the local medical center. Pete, what do you have for us?*"

The camera panned down Tumbleweed Road before zeroing in on a male reporter standing outside of the medi-clinic. "I've spoken to the local coroner who says the victim was a twenty-two-year-old female, a relative newcomer to Lost Trail. While it does appear she died from a blow to the head, this won't be confirmed until the preliminary autopsy report is released, which will probably be later tomorrow."

"Do we know the victim's name?"

"That hasn't been released, pending notification of next of kin. I've talked to a few locals who are under the impression the woman worked as a casual laborer at a local Christmas tree farm."

Tiff tensed as the camera swung into a close-up of the Raven Christmas Tree Farm sign on the side of the road, then panned over the big red barn and the fields of firs, spruces, and pines.

"Apparently, the victim began working here in October, baling Christmas trees and loading them into trucks for delivery to various tree lots in Missoula and neighboring towns."

Next the camera focused on Tiff's family home, zooming in on the porch and the welcoming front door. "We asked to speak to the farm manager as well as the business owner, a Mrs. Rosemary Masterson, but our requests for an interview were denied."

Tiff felt like burying her head in her arms. Why had she heard nothing about this request for an interview? The film crew must have come by shortly after she left for town. She hadn't seen anyone drive up the lane while she was out in the garden.

"Ugh this is awful. I'm sorry for that poor woman. But I hate that our family business is getting this kind of publicity."

"The timing is bad. So close to Christmas. But I wonder if you're onto something with your new manager theory. So far he's the last person who saw her alive. Any idea if Kenny had a relationship with Riley outside of work?"

"Not that he's admitted to us or the sheriff. Ford was out this morning interviewing us, by the way."

Zak nodded. "Yeah. He had me type up his notes."

"Did he find out anything useful? I know he didn't from us—Riley hadn't worked at the farm very long and my aunt and mom hardly knew her—but maybe from the other employees?"

"I can't share confidential information from the office. But let's just say that from what I can tell, the sheriff didn't probe very deeply."

"Maybe he's just going through the motions because he's already made up his mind the killer was someone from Riley's past." Of all the possibilities, it was the most palatable. No one, including Tiff, wanted to think that someone capable of beating a woman to death lived in Lost Trail.

"I can't comment on that. But I sure as hell wish I'd been present when he questioned Riley's co-workers. Maybe they had nothing useful to say. But I wonder. A pretty young woman like Riley, working with five men…"

Tiff could see where he was heading. "You think one of them might have hit on her?"

"It's possible."

"Well I hope it wasn't Bob Jenkins. He's married with two kids." Tiff shuddered at the thought.

"That leaves us with Jacob Bradshaw, Robin Wilson, and Rusty Thurston."

He paused, obviously waiting for her to jump in with her thoughts.

She held up her empty palms. "Sorry, I don't know any of those guys."

"I forget sometimes how long you've been gone. I can fill you in with the basics. Jacob's family owns the Lost Trail ski hill, but he sometimes takes short-term work during off-season. He's in his thirties and married. No kids."

"Speculating wildly here, but say he *did* have a thing with Riley. And then say she threatened to tell his wife about the affair…"

"Yeah. Something like that might be possible."

"What about the other two guys?"

"Robin is young, just graduated from high school this spring. I'd say our more likely candidate is Rusty. He's in his mid-twenties, and known around here for enjoying a good time."

"If either of those guys had been dating Riley, though, they'd have no reason to keep it a secret." Playing armchair detective was a fun intellectual challenge, as long as she didn't think too much about Riley. What she must have suffered. The tragedy of a life cut so short.

Tiff rubbed at a circle of condensation on the table. She'd never met Riley, but the woman had worked for Raven Farm. In her mother's and aunt's eyes, that made her almost like family.

"If you want, I could arrange for you to talk to the guys tomorrow."

Zak looked intrigued. "This would have to be an unofficial visit. I'm just the dispatcher, remember."

"But you just told me you didn't think the sheriff had been very thorough with his questions."

"Which isn't really my place to say."

Tiff studied his eyes closely. She could tell he wanted to do this. "Just come by at noon and I'll give you a tour of the farm. If we happen to catch the guys at lunch, I'm sure the subject of Riley will come up. How could it not?"

Chapter Nine

ALTHOUGH ZAK ARRIVED at the office half an hour earlier than usual, Nadine had beaten him there. She had her head bent over her keyboard and didn't look up when he said good morning.

He immediately felt a twinge of shame. Last night at the bar, he could have been friendlier. After all, Nadine was relatively new in Lost Trail. He didn't know why she got under his skin the way she did. When the sheriff had announced he was hiring her, Zak had watched a few of her barrel races on YouTube. She was amazing. Absolutely fearless. And the bond between her and her horse, Mane Event, had been obvious and beautiful.

Usually his first task of the day was to put on a pot of coffee, but Nadine had beaten him there as well. He swallowed, trying to figure out why he felt resentful rather than grateful.

"Thanks for putting on the coffee."

"Didn't do it for you. I'm on my second cup."

He filled his lungs slowly. "Well, thanks anyway." He settled at his desk, typed in his password. Dozens of new emails popped up on his screen, including one from Cora Christensen.

"Damn, I never did send anyone to check out those vandalism complaints from Halloween."

"How many were there? If I have time I'll take care of it this afternoon."

"Two." He passed her the slips of paper with names, addresses, and details of the complaints. "Watch out for Cora. She seems like a sweet old lady at first, but her strike comes fast and venomous, just like a snake."

"Fine way to talk about an esteemed senior citizen." Nadine's voice was laced with sarcasm, but she also looked curious.

"You meet her, then tell me what you think."

"Will do." Nadine's chair scraped against the wooden floor as she pushed away from her desk. She put on her jacket, tucking a notebook into the pocket. "I've got some more interviews to conduct this morning. So far we haven't found anyone who saw our victim after she left work on Halloween night."

"That doesn't bode well for Kenny Bombard, does it?"

Nadine shrugged. "The sheriff is pretty confident the perp wasn't from Lost Trail. Though that farm manger is relatively new to town also, isn't he?"

"He was hired about six months ago. Lived in Missoula before that."

"I wonder if he could have known Riley previously…?"

Nadine cocked a hip as she considered the question. "Maybe she worked at one of the ski lodges where Kenny was guiding?"

"Doesn't seem likely. But I suppose it's possible."

"I'll check into it after I finish my interviews."

Zak had to curb the automatic impulse to offer to do it instead. Active investigative work wasn't within his work mandate. He'd never had trouble with the limitations of his job before, but he had to admit, they were starting to chafe.

Black cleared her throat. "So. That woman at the bar. She your girlfriend?"

He wasn't sure what surprised him more. The idea of Tiff as his girlfriend. Or the fact that Deputy Black was interested. "Tiff Masterson and I went to school together. She's been working as a CPA in Seattle, but she's home now. Possibly to stay."

"I assume she's related to the woman who owns the Raven Christmas Tree Farm?"

"Yes. She's Rosemary's daughter."

"What's the family story there? What happened to the father?"

"It's pretty tragic. Tiff's older brother, Casey, was born with a severe congenital heart defect. He was scheduled for surgery when he was twelve, but he didn't make it. A few months later, their dad died in car accident, leaving just Tiff and her mother."

Nadine compressed her lips while she thought about this.

Then she asked, "Any chance the dad's death wasn't an accident?"

Zak narrowed his eyes. "What are you suggesting?"

"A death like that following so soon after the loss of a son…surely suicide has to be a consideration."

"Maybe. Except his wife and sister-in-law were in the vehicle with him. Between them they were all the family his daughter Tiff had. What kind of father would risk leaving a ten-year-old child alone in the world?"

"Point taken," she said but she didn't sound convinced.

Zak was tempted to pull out the file and prove her wrong. But older cases were locked up in the basement and they had enough real work to do today. Better to stay focused on that.

BY NOON, ROSEMARY still wasn't out of bed, and Tiff wasn't sure if she should be concerned. Her aunt was working today, and Zak would be here soon. She decided to wait until after Zak left to check in on her mom. Tiff made egg salad sandwiches and met Zak at the front door when she heard his truck drive up.

The November air had a bite, so she pulled on one of her aunt's heavier coats. After years of living in Seattle her wardrobe was definitely inadequate for the upcoming Montana winter. She'd have to do some online shopping soon…which reminded her of the unhappy state of her bank account.

Later this afternoon she had to talk to her mom about her business idea.

Zak stepped out of the car, and immediately his light brown hair was whipped up by the wind. He wasn't a tall man and with his light runner's build and pleasant but unremarkable features, he'd never been the type of guy to stand out in a crowd.

That fact had never seemed to bother him, though. In fact Tiff suspected he liked blending in.

When he was close enough she handed him a sandwich. "Lunch. You okay to eat while we walk to the barn?" A tidy, woodchip-lined path led the way, little more than a football field's length away from the house.

"Hell yeah. Thanks for this. The bread looks home-made."

"You know my mother."

"I'd forgotten, but now that you mention it… Any chance I can score some cookies later?"

"That won't be a problem." She only hoped that if her mom was awake by then, she'd also be dressed and in a somewhat presentable state.

Zak fell into step beside her, and as they were both around eight inches above five feet their strides matched almost perfectly. Zak had his sandwich finished in about five bites, or so it seemed to Tiff. He certainly had a healthy appetite.

"I'm sorry I've forgotten to ask before, but how is your family?" She broached the question carefully. Zak had never been one to discuss problems at home, but she knew there had been some. His father, normally a gregarious and charming man, had a town-wide reputation for being a mean drunk.

She knew from her aunt that the older Waller boys, and sometimes their mother, had been taken to the clinic many times with suspicious injuries. A few times Child Welfare had been called in, but somehow the Wallers always smoothed things over.

She wasn't sure if Zak, himself, had ever been physically abused at home. He'd never talked about it with her. And yet she suspected that as the youngest of four boys in a rough-and-tumble household, he'd perfected the talent of making himself almost invisible as a survival technique.

"After my father liquidated his store, it was a pretty ugly scene for a while, as he began drinking pretty heavily. Then my mom's father died and left her some property, a grain farm in South Dakota. They moved a few years ago. Dad's going to try and make a go of it. My brothers Curtis and Jake went with them. And Matt signed up for the army."

"So you're the only Waller left in Lost Trail."

"Yup," he said cheerfully.

They were at the barn then, and Zak paused to take in the view. "Impressive place. I remember when we used to play hide-and-seek in here."

"Lots of nooks and crannies." She'd played with her brother, too, though Dad was always cautioning them not to run too much. "Did you and your family ever come out at Christmas time?"

"Never. We had an artificial tree. Dad special ordered it when I was just a kid. It was white and silver." He noticed her shocked expression and chuckled. "I thought it was god-awful, too, but Mom was glad she didn't have to water it or clean up a mess of needles when she took it down."

"In my family admitting you have an artificial tree is on par with saying you don't like puppies or kittens. Honestly, Zak, nothing makes a house smell like Christmas more than a fresh-cut pine tree."

"I guess love of Christmas trees must be in your blood." He scanned the area around the barn. "So where is all the staff?"

"They'll be inside, eating lunch. That's why I suggested you come at this time."

"Smart woman." He followed her toward the door, but paused before entering. "This barn is in great shape. When was it built?"

"My great-grandfather built the original during the Depression. Every generation since has made their own improvements. My grandfather added a large bathroom and a mini kitchen for the staff, while my father upgraded all the public areas, including an indoor fireplace with a seating area for customers to enjoy their apple ciders and home-baked cookies."

In the city when she told people her family owned a Christmas tree farm in Montana, she was met with disbelief. When she asked them where they thought their trees came from, most just shrugged and admitted they'd never thought about it.

But Tiff was proud of the family business, and the way they'd weathered the various economic highs and lows of the past eighty-odd years. The idea of a farm where you grow Christmas trees might seem all Norman Rockwell to some people, but she knew it took a lot of planning, hard work, and smarts to make a business like this survive for so long.

The main door was on a track and Zak pushed the paneled door open so they could go inside. Tiff guided him through the public gathering area, pointed out the store where she and her brother had worked so proudly, then led him into the kitchen area.

Here, as she'd expected, they found the workers. Only Kenny was missing from the group sitting at the rectangular wooden table, eating their various packed lunches. They'd been chatting companionably when she opened the door, but now they fell silent.

"Hey, Bob." She greeted the eldest man at the table, the only one she recognized. In his forties now, Bob was a heavyset man, with a dark complexion and rough, slightly oversized features.

"Hi, Tiff. I heard you'd come home again. Let me introduce the guys…"

Bob said the names so quickly, Tiff wouldn't have kept them straight if Zak hadn't already prepped her. Robin Wilson was a tall, gangly youth, still battling acne, and too shy to look her straight in the eyes.

Jacob Bradshaw, the married guy in his thirties, had a thick, dark beard and a calm, assured manner. If he was hiding any secrets, he was doing so masterfully.

Belying his fun-loving nature, the third guy Bob introduced—Rusty Thurston—looked like he had a weight on his mind. He was clean-shaven, with several ear piercings and a tatt covering one side of his neck.

"So, Zak, what brings you out here?" Bob asked, once the introductions were over.

"Haven't been here since I was a kid. Tiff's giving me a tour of the place. I guess it's busy season for you guys, huh?"

"Sure is, but it's been hard to focus the last few days," Bob said. "We can't stop thinking about that kid, Riley."

"She was way too young to die," Jacob agreed.

"She didn't die. She was murdered," corrected Rusty.

"She was such a little thing. Must have been one sick bastard," Jacob said.

Everyone nodded and after a pause, Tiff asked another question. "Did she ever talk about friends, or guys in her life?"

"Nope. She said she was done with romance. Made me

laugh, since she was so young and all," Bob said.

"We teased her, and sometimes we could make her laugh," Rusty added. "But mostly she was quiet. We tried inviting her to the bar after work on Fridays but she always said no."

"She was small," added Bob. "But she was tough. And a hard worker."

The men all nodded.

Zak raised his eyebrows at Tiff and she realized he wanted her to keep asking questions. "Where did Riley live?"

"It was pretty obvious she was sleeping in her car," Jacob said.

"That's right," Rusty said. "I called her on it one day and she admitted it. But with the weather getting colder, she realized that wasn't going to work much longer. My buddy and I have an extra bedroom in the house we're renting. Riley was going to move in November first, after payday."

"You have an ulterior motive in offering her a bedroom?" Zak asked. "She was pretty cute, right?"

Rusty gave a good-natured shrug. "Hell, I admit I hit on her. She let me down easy, though."

"And that didn't affect her decision to move in with you?"

"It was a strictly roommate agreement. She'd even paid us a month's rent. What should I do with the money?"

"I wouldn't worry about that right now," Zak said. "So far we haven't found any next of kin. Did she ever talk about her life back in California?"

"Nope. That kid didn't talk about anything." Bob got up from the table and threw his sandwich wrapper in the trash.

"Except TV shows," Robin said quietly, speaking up for the first time. "We were working together last week and she couldn't stop talking about *Orange is the New Black*."

"Where could she have watched TV shows?" Tiff wondered. Living in a car, Riley wouldn't have access to Wi-Fi.

"I don't know," Robin admitted.

"She had to hang out somewhere when she wasn't at work," Tiff said. "Do you guys have any ideas where she went?"

Everyone looked blank and then a sound at the door caused them all to turn. In strode Kenny, yanking off his work gloves. "Damn but it's cold out there today."

Immediately the men put away the last of their lunches and began filing out to resume work. Unperturbed, Kenny went to the fridge and pulled out a big, meaty sandwich.

"How long do the guys usually take for lunch?" Tiff wondered if they'd gone over their allotted time, or if they just preferred to avoid their boss.

"Thirty minutes usually. Nothing's been on schedule since we heard the news about Riley, though." Kenny went to Zak and held out his hand. "Don't think we've met. I'm Kenny Bombard."

"Good to meet you. I'm Zak Waller. Tiff and I went to school together."

It was an interesting contrast seeing the two men standing next to one another. Kenny was probably only three or four inches taller than Zak but with his athletic, muscular build, he made her poor friend look like a bit of a weakling. To his credit though, Zak didn't seem intimidated.

"So what's up?" Kenny asked casually, glancing from Zak to Tiff.

"Zak's an old friend. I was just giving him a tour of the barn."

"Is that right?" Kenny turned back to Zak, his eyes narrowed and voice measured. "So where is it you work, Zak?"

"Dispatcher for the sheriff's office. Speaking of which, I ought to get back. Thanks for the tour, Tiff. Maybe I'll buy a real tree this Christmas."

Chapter Ten

"HAVE YOU FINISHED your preliminary autopsy, Dad?" Justin asked, after the server, a young man named Cody, took their dinner orders.

Justin and his father had been going to Lolo's Pizza on Thursday nights ever since Justin's mother died when he was only six. Franny always had a weak constitution was what people often said about his mother.

His father, however, was still going strong at fifty-nine. As the town's only doctor, Clark Pittman worked long hours at the clinic in addition to his duties as the local coroner.

"I have. Stopped in at the sheriff's office on my way here. Ford was just about to give a statement to the press."

"Was it pretty conclusive?"

"I can't say yet if she had any alcohol or drugs in her system, but the cause of death is straightforward enough. Subdural hematoma with resulting cerebellar tonsillar herniation and brain stem compression."

Used to his father's medical jargon, Justin rolled with it. "Caused by a blow to the head?"

"Two blows actually. I'd say the first was the result of a

right-handed punch from a very strong male, which probably rendered her immediately unconscious. He must have hit her quickly with a second punch, before she collapsed."

Justin winced. "Do they have any idea who did it?"

"None. The woman was new to town. Didn't know many people other than her co-workers at Raven Farm. But apparently they didn't socialize outside of work."

"To be killed like that…someone must have really hated her."

"Or else someone must have really loved her, which amounts to the same thing in extreme cases."

Justin grimaced. "I hope they find the bastard. Do you think Sheriff Ford is up to the job?"

His father cleared his throat. "You know my views on Archie Ford. All he cares about is getting re-elected. He's already figured out it'll be best for him and the community if he can pin the death on someone from the victim's past. Someone with no connection to Lost Trail."

"That's a theory that can let us all sleep soundly tonight."

"Exactly."

Justin glanced out the window. The road and sidewalks were quiet now, but for most of the day there'd been a TV crew from Missoula, and another from Helena, trying to dig up news on the homicide. This was not the sort of publicity Sheriff Ford would want for his county. "But I hope the sheriff's office is still going to investigate other possibilities."

"What? That someone from this town killed her?" Clark

shook his head. "My guess is Ford and Butterfield will go through the motions of asking around town, and then try to shuck this off to the victim's home state of California as soon as they can."

"What about that new deputy they hired? She looks pretty capable."

"Yeah, but she'll have Ford fighting every move she makes if she steps out of line. It's too bad about Zak."

"What do you mean?"

"Zak Waller is a bright man, with a good heart, who had the bad luck to be born to the wrong family. His dad and older brothers were pretty rough. I'd like to see him take some initiative in the sheriff's office—but I'm afraid he'll never have the balls to stand up to our sheriff."

Cody came with their pizzas then, and for a few minutes Justin and his dad concentrated on eating.

After their first slices were gone, Clark downed a long drink of beer. "Marsha was working at the clinic today. She told me Tiff has come back to town. Marsha thinks it's more than a visit."

Justin put down his fork. "Yeah, I've heard and I'm surprised. Things seemed to be going so well for her when we visited her in Seattle last fall."

Lost Trail sure didn't have much to offer a university-educated woman like Tiff. If not for his father, Justin sure wouldn't be living here. But when he was growing up his father had always been there for him. And he'd been so delighted when Justin suggested he might start his own law practice in Lost Trail that Justin had been compelled to follow through.

"Lots of kids crave the big city. A few years of pollution, miserable traffic, and long commutes is the best cure."

"I don't think Tiff wanted the big city life as much as to leave the place her brother and father died."

"Bad things happen everywhere. And you can't get over a broken heart by changing your address."

His father's philosophy explained why he hadn't moved after his own wife's death. When he was a kid Justin had taken his father's widowed status for granted. As an adult, though, Justin wondered if his father ever considered remarrying. He seemed to have a close relationship with Marsha Holmes.

Marsha was only a few years younger, intelligent, attractive, and Justin knew his father respected her abilities at work. Yet the few times Justin had hinted about the possibility of a romance, his father had practically shuddered.

For a few minutes they ate in silence, Justin enjoying his vegetarian pizza on a thin crust and his dad chowing down on his deep-dish meat-lovers.

"So how are your new wife and daughter doing? They could join us on Thursday nights, you know. This isn't a sacrosanct father-son thing."

"I appreciate that, Dad. Maybe next week." Having a wife and child was so new to him. But his father was right. It was up to him to blend the new family with the old, even though Willow and his father had never gotten along very well. Willow found his father stodgy, while Clark had never approved of Willow's adventurous spirit. But now that Willow was his wife, he hoped they would both make an effort.

The one common bond among them all was Geneva. His dad was as thrilled to be a grandfather as Justin was to be a dad.

"Is Willow planning to find a job? I imagine she finds it dull being a stay-at-home mom."

"She'd like to next year, when Geneva starts kindergarten."

"What sort of work does she do?"

Justin chose his words carefully. "She studied general arts in college. Majored in Women's Studies. And she's a talented amateur photographer."

His father maintained a neutral expression. "Not too many jobs in Lost Trail for people with those qualifications."

"No." Especially not for one who had graduated ten years ago and hadn't held a steady job since.

Justin had pruned and shaped his history with Willow to make his sudden marriage more understandable for his dad. He'd invented a college romance, elevating Willow from one of his best friends, to his lover.

The truth was he and Willow had spent almost all their time hanging out with his first-year roommate Paul Quinlan.

Paul was a guy of great charm and intellect, a student of philosophy from a family of seemingly unlimited means. For most of the four years of Justin's undergraduate degree the three of them had been inseparable.

But while there'd been an attraction back then, it had never been acted upon.

After graduation they hadn't drifted apart, it had been more of a violent rupture. Paul and Willow had wanted to travel, while Justin, having been accepted into law, remained in Missoula. Neither Paul nor Willow were much for email or social media so he couldn't even follow them that way. When Willow showed up at his door six months ago, with Geneva asleep in the backseat of her car, he hadn't seen her for almost ten years.

Yet he'd taken her in. And been glad to do it. He wouldn't have dared suggest marriage if Willow hadn't brought it up first, along with the idea of adopting Geneva. Pushing his qualms aside, he'd immediately said yes. This might be his only chance to have a family. He didn't dare risk losing it.

But fate had the last laugh. Just that morning in the shower, Justin had felt another swelling.

TIFF DROVE ALONG Lost Creek Road slowly, jittery at the prospect of her upcoming visit. The most luxurious homes in

Lost Trail were here on the west side of town bordering the creek, with unobstructed views of the magnificent Bitterroot Mountains.

The largest home of all, at the far end of the road, belonged to Jen and Will Sparks, Derick's parents. Tiff had visited him a few times there, back in her tutoring days, and she'd been awed by the expensive furnishings and the way Derick could control everything—raising and lowering of blinds, the house temperature, the music playing on the built-in speaker system—with his mother's remote control.

Derick's mother had served the kind of snacks Tiff craved. Not homemade cookies, which were always in ample supply at home, but bags of potato chips and sodas in a tempting array of flavors. Mrs. Sparks always fussed over Tiff. No doubt she was anxious to see her son graduate high school, and she saw Tiff's help as necessary for that plan.

But despite all the perks and the nice treatment, Tiff had never felt comfortable in that house. Mrs. Sparks had been a hoverer. And behind her smile, sparked an occasional sharpness Tiff never saw in either of her parents.

Knowing Derick now worked at the family construction business, it seemed strange that he would have chosen to live on the same street as his parents, and only four doors down. How did Aubrey feel about having her in-laws such an integral part of her married life? Tiff doubted if she would want her own in-laws to be so close.

After checking the address on her phone, Tiff pulled into

the spacious driveway of the three-car garage.

Derick and Aubrey's home wasn't as big as his parents', but it had to be at least four thousand square feet. She hoped they were planning on adopting a lot more children.

She grabbed the baby gift she'd purchased in Hamilton that afternoon and then got out of her vehicle, not bothering to lock it. It was five after seven, hopefully Derick and Aubrey would be finished with dinner, which was when Derick had texted would be the best time to drop in.

But as she approached the portico and the massive double doors she could hear an argument. Unsure what to do, she lingered for a few minutes as the voices see-sawed from Derick's, low but insistent, to Aubrey's, high-pitched and almost hysterical.

Every couple had disagreements, but this sounded intense. Apparently the marital problems that had preceded the arrival of the baby had returned. Tiff was about to retreat to her car, when she heard Derick say her name. Up until then she hadn't made out any of the conversation, but there was no doubting the cadence of *Tiffany Masterson*. A moment later she saw a shadow at the front window, and after a pause of almost thirty seconds, the front door opened.

Derick gave her the fakest smile ever. "Hey, Tiff. Good to see you."

They didn't hug. They'd never been the kind of friends who did that.

"You, too. Fatherhood must agree with you."

Actually, he didn't look well. He'd been a big, solid guy in high school, but he'd gained weight around his middle, and though he was only thirty, his light brown hair had begun to thin. Judging by the shadows under his eyes, he hadn't been sleeping much lately.

The new baby? Or troubles with Aubrey? Either one, or both, must be keeping him up at night.

"Sorry if I picked a bad time. I just wanted to drop off this baby gift." She held up the pretty yellow and green gift bag as proof.

Aubrey appeared in the doorway then, coming up beside her husband, who wrapped his arm around her shoulders. The girl Tiff remembered as so pretty from high school looked almost plain today. The puffy skin around her pink-tinged eyes suggested she'd been crying. The baggy black sweatshirt she was wearing over dark leggings was smeared with what Tiff guessed was baby vomit. For the final insult, Aubrey's hair, which had been a glossy red ten years ago, was now darker and duller, pulled into a harsh ponytail.

"Hey, Tiffany, I didn't know you were back in town."

Tiff bit back her usually automatic correction of her name. "I've only been here a few days. Congratulations on your new baby."

Derick turned to his wife, who was quick to reply, "Thanks. I wish we could invite you in to meet Brody but we just got him to sleep. Besides, the house is a mess."

The portion Tiff could see—a large foyer with maple

plank flooring leading to an open-concept family room— looked immaculate. "That's okay. I should have called first."

Derick flushed and glanced away. As she'd suspected he didn't want to admit that he'd replied to her earlier message with an invitation to drop by that evening.

"Thanks for coming by, Tiffany. It was really sweet of you." Aubrey put her hand on the door.

"Let me give you this at least."

As Aubrey leaned forward to accept the gift bag, the late evening sun slanted over her face, revealing a faint greenish bruise on her cheekbone.

"Thanks, Tiffany."

"My pleasure." She glanced pointedly at the bruise. "That looks nasty."

Derick's face paled, but Aubrey gave a weak laugh. "Yeah, I forgot to open my eyes one night when I got up to feed Brody. Ran right into our bedroom door."

That had to be the lamest excuse in the world. But Tiff couldn't imagine another scenario—certainly Derick wasn't the type to hit his wife—so maybe it was true.

Chapter Eleven

THOUGH IT WAS only seven-thirty when Tiff returned home, her mother had already retired to her small room over the garage. Tiff considered going up to wish her good night, but the aroma of popcorn lured her to the family room where her aunt was watching an episode of *The Fall*. Marsha was on the sofa, with her feet up on a stool and a big bowl of popcorn on her lap.

"Come and join me."

Tiff sank onto the sofa, then reached for a handful of popcorn, her attention on the screen. "I loved that series. It's so intense. This is from the second season, right?"

"Yes. It's almost over."

Tiff was easily immersed in the story and they watched until the credits rolled. Marsha powered off the TV and turned sideways against the arm of the sofa so it was easier to talk.

"How was your visit with Derick and Aubrey? I didn't expect you back so soon. You must have barely crossed the threshold."

"I didn't get that far." Tiff relayed an abbreviated version of her conversation with Derick and Aubrey—omitting Aubrey's bruise and her own questions about what had caused it. "Obviously I caught them at a bad time. But Derick made it sound as if everything between them was perfect since they adopted Brody."

"Maybe now that the initial excitement has worn off they've realized how much work it is to have a baby."

"That must be it." And yet what she'd overheard hadn't sounded like a squabble over baby chores, or frayed nerves.

"The Sparks family are used to having life go their way. They have a successful, lucrative business, can afford luxury vacations and live in the best homes in the county. Babies can be very inconvenient when you're used to having what you want, when you want it. Mark my words—they'll hire a nanny within the next month."

"Derick gave me the impression Aubrey wants to be a stay-at-home mom."

"I'm sure she does. But will she be willing to give up her pamper days at the spa, and her shopping excursions with her mother-in-law?"

"You sound like you know the Sparks family well."

"When you work at the only medical clinic in town you get to know *everyone*. It's common knowledge Aubrey tried for years to get pregnant without success. I can tell you that without violating confidentiality."

"Yes, Derick said." She hesitated. "The problem was with him—low sperm count."

Her aunt raised her eyebrows. "I suspected that much. Will's brother and wife—they live in Missoula—also ended up having to adopt. Fertility is one problem money can't always fix."

"Derick wasn't adopted was he?"

"No. I remember when Jen was pregnant. She hated it. She never worried if her baby would be born healthy with all his fingers and toes like most mothers. All she cared about was her figure and whether she'd look the same after the baby."

"Are you and Jen Sparks the same age?"

"We are. In fact we were best of friends for years, until Jen—she was a Wheeler back then—set her sights on marrying Will Sparks. That man never had a chance."

"Did Mom have a best friend as well?"

"Sybil Tombe. They were both in the school year behind me."

Sybil had been operating the local library for as long as Tiff could remember. She was a lovely lady and while Tiff had known she and her mom were friends, she hadn't realized once they'd been so close.

Tiff ate another scoop of popcorn, then went to the kitchen. "Want some sparkling water, Aunt Marsha?"

"Sure. With ice and lemon if you don't mind."

When Tiff returned, she handed her aunt a glass, then settled back into the same spot. "I've been thinking about staying in Lost Trail. Opening my own accounting practice."

Her aunt stopped mid-sip and began to cough. After a few moments, she managed a deep breath. "Sorry about that. Too many bubbles." She set down her glass. "Your mother would love to have you living here again. So would I, to be honest. But are you making this decision for the right reasons? You were always anxious to spread your wings. And you're doing so well with your firm. Two promotions in seven years. You should be proud."

It was time to tell her aunt the entire story. "Things haven't been good recently. Shortly after Christmas I started having these anxiety attacks, trouble sleeping at night." It was embarrassing to admit to behavior so much like her mother's, but she couldn't keep the truth hidden anymore. "Because I was so tired, I began sleeping in, being late for work. During tax season this spring I missed a couple of important deadlines. Then in May I was late for an audit committee meeting for one of the firm's biggest and most important clients."

She glanced at the glass in her hands, unable to continue to meet her aunt's troubled gaze. "I was let go from the firm the second week of May. That same week Craig broke up with me. He said I had changed and I couldn't argue. I had."

"Oh, honey." Marsha laid a compassionate hand on her shoulder. "What happened to bring on those anxiety attacks?"

"That's just it, I don't know." The only event she could recall from that period was a visit from Dr. Pittman and

Justin. They'd been in Seattle for business reasons and claimed they couldn't go home without taking her out for dinner.

But that dinner couldn't possibly have been the trigger for her subsequent anxiety attacks. She'd had such a nice time with them. She'd known Dr. Pittman all her life and gorgeous Justin had been her mentor in her AP Literature class. While he was helping her learn to write term papers they'd discovered a shared love of American authors from the thirties and forties: Steinbeck, Fitzgerald, Hemmingway.

Her friends had all been so jealous. Blond-haired Justin, with his chiseled features and ripped physique, had been almost everyone's crush back then.

The night they'd gone for dinner in Seattle, though, he'd seemed paler than usual, almost drawn. He was wearing his blond hair cropped now, a style that suggested he might be suffering from premature balding. Dr. Pittman entertained them with stories about his childhood and about courting Justin's mother, Franny.

The only false step in the entire evening was when Tiff asked how Franny had died. She'd been a toddler when it happened, and couldn't remember her folks ever talking about it.

"She had a weak constitution," Justin said quietly. "She got the flu after Christmas, when I was six, and her heart just gave out on her."

From that moment on, the life went out of the evening.

They finished their desserts in silence and then the men had dropped Tiff off at her apartment before heading for a hotel near the airport to expedite their early morning flight to Montana.

"The day after I was fired I bought a backpack and a ticket to Argentina. I've spent the past six months traveling," Tiff admitted. "And I've pretty much depleted my savings. I was hoping if I started a business here Raven Farm would be my first client."

"We need to consult your mother, but I can't imagine her saying anything but yes. I'm sure she'd be delighted to have you working at the family business."

It was very polite of Marsha to pretend her mother still ran the farm, when they both knew Marsha had made the majority of the decisions since Tiff's dad died.

"There's no way I could ever thank you enough for all you do for this family." She never could have left her mother, gone to college, worked in Seattle, if she hadn't had Aunt Marsha to rely upon. "Not many sisters would have done as much as you've done for Mom."

Marsha had basically given up her own personal life to move in with her sister and help with Rosemary's business and daughter, caring for them both as if they were her own.

"It hasn't been a sacrifice. Rosemary is my only sibling. How could I watch her suffer and not help? Besides, I've had a job I love. And while I may not have had children, I've certainly enjoyed having a very special niece."

They weren't normally a physically affectionate family, but Tiff felt the moment called for a hug. Her aunt went stiff for a moment, then returned the embrace.

"You make your family proud, Tiff. I just hope you don't regret your decision to leave Seattle. Much as your mom would love having you nearby, she wants the best for you."

"Maybe it's cowardly, running home after my first setback. But I feel this is where I need to be right now."

And despite the bad memories and her fractured relationship with her mother, Tiff did love this place. Somewhere deep inside of her, the landscape of Lost Trail and Raven Farm had taken root and become her ideal of what home looked and smelled and felt like.

"Just know that if you change your mind, you're free to follow your dreams wherever they may lead you. Your mom and I are doing just fine here."

Tiff wished she could believe her. But this life of her mother's, nights of insomnia followed by foggy days with only a few productive hours of baking or gardening…it seemed more like surviving than living.

"Do you think Mom will ever go back to the way she was…before?" Tiff's memories of a laughing, energetic mother, one who embraced life and was always up for a new adventure—whether it was an impromptu picnic on Huckleberry Hill or a surprise camping trip in Yellowstone—were becoming dimmer with each year.

"I had hope at one time. But…she's getting older, Tiff. Set in a pattern."

"Did she ever go for psychiatric help?"

"You know she had to be hospitalized the month after your father died. Then about two years after that, when she was showing no interest in resuming any semblance of her former life, Clark referred her to a specialist in Missoula. Rosemary went to a few appointments with the specialist. But after a month she told me she was done. I've never been able to convince her to try someone else."

"Is she on any medications?"

"She gets a lorazepam on nights when she's having a harder time than usual falling asleep. I usually give it to her at night with her herbal tea. Sometimes she takes antidepressants, when she's feeling especially down."

"Are there long-term implications to taking those drugs?"

"Potentially. But I'm very careful with the doses."

Tiff felt suddenly weighed down with exhaustion. "I'm going to turn in, Aunt Marsha. See you in the morning."

"Sleep tight, honey."

Tiff carried the popcorn bowl and glasses to the kitchen. The dishwasher was running so she washed them by hand and left them to dry. She could hear the next episode from *The Fall* start in the family room as she made her way up the stairs.

At the top of the landing she paused. A faint light shone under her mother's door. She took a deep breath then, after a faint knock on the door, went in to say good night.

The only light was the reading lamp beside her mother's bed. Next to the lamp were the school photos of herself and her brother, taken when they were ten and twelve respectively. Her brother hadn't lived to have another school photo, but she had.

And yet her mother had never updated the picture in that frame.

Her mother was propped up in bed, reading a book with a pretty cover of a couple standing on a street corner, with silver snowflakes all around them. She let the book fall flat when she saw Tiff.

"Sweetie. You look so pretty. Were you out?"

"Just dropped in on Derick and Aubrey to see the new baby."

"Is the baby cute?"

"I can't say. He was sleeping so I wasn't invited in. I guess I didn't pick a good time to visit."

"That's too bad." Her mother patted a spot on her bed and Tiff sat down.

"What are you reading?"

"It's supposed to be a lovely story from one of my favorite authors. Sybil was kind enough to bring it by the other day. But I keep reading the same page over and over... Maybe I'll try again tomorrow."

Her mother's eyes looked small and old, the pretty blue of her irises blurred by a sheen of moisture. Now was not the time to talk about her plans…or to confess what had really brought her home.

"I'll let you sleep then. Good night, Mom." She dropped a kiss on her mother's forehead. "I love you."

Chapter Twelve

Z AK WAS SURPRISED when Justin Pittman showed up unannounced early Friday morning. Justin had changed subtly in the past year, become thinner and gaunter, and he'd started shaving his blond hair. Still, he remained the most handsome man in Lost Trail. Until his quick marriage to Willow a few months ago, he'd definitely been the most eligible.

"Hey, Zak."

"Justin. What brings you to the sheriff's office this morning?"

"I've been thinking about that young woman who was killed. It occurred to me that a short meeting I had with her once might be of interest to whoever is investigating…" Justin's gaze roamed the rest of the room, pausing on Nadine who was the only other person who'd managed to make it to work so far.

Nadine had been watching him with interest since he'd entered. No doubt she was checking out his baby blues and his pumped-up muscles, barely concealed by the slim tailoring of his pants and sports jacket.

"I can take your statement." She waved him over.

"We meet again. No crime scene tape this time." Justin offered his hand and Nadine shook it.

"Sorry about that. Standard operating procedure when we have an unexplained death."

"No worries," Justin said, though his expression suggested otherwise. A moment later his smile broadened. "How are you liking Lost Trail. From what my father says, you're just what this town needs."

At his desk Zak rolled his eyes. Yup, turn on the flattery. With guys like Justin it always worked.

"It's a good job. I was glad to get it." She pulled out her notebook. "So you're a lawyer, right? Where's your office?"

"Above the dentist's, next to the Snowdrift Café."

"They have amazing muffins at that café."

"So you're figuring out all the local hot spots. That's good. I trust you've been to the Dew Drop Inn?"

"We're intimately acquainted."

As they shared a laugh, Zak wondered if Nadine had even noticed the sparkling new wedding band on Pittman's left hand. Maybe she had, because she finally got down to business.

"So I heard you talking to Zak at the front desk. You said you had a recent meeting with Riley Concurran?"

"Yes. She dropped by two Fridays ago just as I was about to lock up for the weekend."

"Had you met her before?"

"No. This was the first I'd seen her, and I was taken aback because this is a small town and I don't often get strangers dropping in. She was very abrupt. I'd no sooner introduced myself than she asked how much my rates were."

"Did she give her name?"

"No. I only realized who she was when I saw her picture on the morning news today. Based on the way she was dressed—her clothes looked like someone else's cast-offs—I told her I sometimes work pro bono. She looked confused so I explained that meant I sometimes helped my clients without expecting payment."

"Okay. Good. What did she do then?"

"She asked me something very odd. She said, 'If someone committed a crime and came to you, would you tell the police?'"

"Interesting. And you said—?"

"Not unless someone was in imminent danger of harm."

"And did that reassure her?"

"Apparently not because she took off. I tried to follow her, but she was fast. The next time I saw her was at least several days later. She was coming out of the library carrying a book. As soon as she saw me she ran in the opposite direction."

"During that first meeting—did she give you any hint what sort of crime she might be talking about?"

"None at all."

"Did she appear frightened?"

"Maybe. She was definitely agitated. I'd say more nervous than scared."

Zak could tell Nadine was lapping up the story word-for-word. Zak, however, was skeptical.

Around this town Justin and his father were treated like royalty. They had money, were well educated, and had deep family roots. Dr. Pittman's grandparents had been one of the original three families who founded Lost Trail.

In school Justin had been two grades ahead of Zak. He'd been the guy every other male student wished he could be, the guy every girl wanted to date. Smart, athletic, and good-looking, Justin Pittman had it all. Most surprisingly of all, he didn't appear to lord his superiority over others, which made him even more popular with adults and kids alike.

When he'd moved home after earning his law degree to hang up his shingle in Lost Trail, everyone talked about what a devoted son he was. The fact that he was the only lawyer in a sixty-mile radius, and would pretty much have the market cornered for business, was never mentioned.

Zak didn't buy the sappy reunited-high-school-lovers story circulating town since Justin and Willow's marriage either. It astounded him that no one else seemed to find it strange for Willow to show up in Lost Trail more than ten years after she'd left, and within weeks, marry Justin and have him adopt her child.

Something was wrong. But Zak couldn't put his finger on it. The entire town might believe Clark and Justin

Pittman were demi-gods. But no one was that perfect. There had to be flaws.

Zak's inability to find even one hadn't stopped him from believing it existed.

Take this story of Justin's about Riley, for instance. Maybe it was all true. Or possibly Riley had come to Justin's office for a more nefarious reason. Knowing there might be witnesses who had seen her either entering or exiting his office, Justin could have put together this story to try and shift attention from him—and to stop anyone from speculating why a pretty, twenty-two-year-old woman would spend a period of time in his office.

But he could tell Nadine was taking every word at face value.

JUSTIN LEFT THE sheriff's office intending to go to work. Instead he picked up a large latte and two apple-cinnamon muffins from the Snowdrift Café and walked the three blocks home. The little bungalow he'd purchased when he'd moved back to open his law practice had seemed fine at the time, especially after he'd renovated the kitchen and bathroom. Now that he was a married man with a child, though, the space was barely adequate. He needed to talk to Willow about moving.

There were lots of things he and Willow needed to talk

about. But every time he broached a subject more serious than what to have for dinner, she retreated.

Fortunately he was a patient man. Eventually she'd be ready to talk. In the meantime it might help if he tried to act more like a newlywed himself.

He went in the front way, through the small foyer to the living room on his left. Geneva was sitting on the sofa, wide-eyed and solemn, watching *Dora the Explorer*.

When she gazed up at him he kissed the top of her head. "Shhh. I have a surprise for Mommy. There's one for you too."

Her gaze moved to the cup and paper bag in his hands and she nodded. A second later, her attention was back on her show.

He hesitated, wishing she was doing something more active. Willow allowed her daughter—their daughter—a lot more screen time than he liked. But he was new to this dad stuff and didn't want to be heavy-handed with his ideas.

From the foyer, a hallway on the right led to the two bedrooms and a bathroom. Straight ahead was the eating alcove, with the kitchen to the left. As he moved away from the TV he could hear Willow talking on her phone.

He held out the coffee as he passed through the arched doorway. Willow was at the far counter, looking out the window, so she didn't see him. She had her phone to her ear and seemed to be listening intently. Just as he was about to clear his throat so she would notice him, she started talking again.

"Well I did marry him so it's—"

He set the cup and bag on the counter and she stopped talking, swirling around, eyes opening wide.

"Justin."

He didn't know what to say. He was trying to process what he'd overheard, even while knowing the words hadn't been meant for his ears.

Willow said a hurried farewell and disconnected the call. "That was an old friend. She's upset I moved to Lost Trail."

"No need to explain. I shouldn't have snuck up on you. I just wanted to bring you a little treat to brighten your morning." He handed her the coffee and muffins. "From the Snowdrift."

Willow's smile was his reward. It was almost like the ones she'd tossed around so easily when they were younger.

"You're sweet. Thank you." She kissed him on the cheek, then opened the bag. "Yum, apple-cinnamon. That's Geneva's favorite flavor." She glanced up at him, tilting her head to one side. "But of course you knew that. You're a pretty special guy, Justin."

"Just want my girls to be happy. But now I should dash back to work. Should I pick up pizza on my way home? It is Friday night. We could watch a movie." It wasn't much to offer, but the recreational choices in Lost Trail were limited, especially when you had a four-year-old child.

"Sure. That would be great."

Justin left the house with a smile, but soon his earlier sense of unease was back and worse than ever. He and Willow were so good at superficial chatter, but one of them had to have the courage to break through and talk about something real for a change. Like that phone call. And the truth about who was on the other end of the line.

Chapter Thirteen

TIFF WAS LAZILY enjoying her second coffee of the day when her aunt returned from her morning yoga session in the basement of the Anglican church.

"Something I meant to tell you last night," her aunt said as she threw the dregs from the pot down the sink and started a fresh brew. "Kenny and I usually have a meeting here at noon on Fridays. Over sandwiches and coffee I sign checks and he fills me in on farm business. How would you like to join us today?"

So Kenny had lunch here every week. No wonder he felt so at home in this kitchen. Tiff tried to squash her lingering resentment toward the man. He was just doing his job.

"I don't remember you having those meetings with Ed."

"I used to meet him at the office in the barn. With Kenny I thought it was time to set up a new routine, one that was more convenient for myself—not to mention your mom. This way, if Rosemary feels up to it, she can always join in."

But did she ever feel up to it? Tiff doubted it. "I'd be glad to sit in today. Want me to help make the sandwiches?"

"That would be great. This will be the perfect time to tell

Kenny you're going to take over the accounting for the farm."

"She is?" Rosemary stepped into the room, dressed in her housecoat, with her hair up in a messy bun. She looked from her sister to her daughter. "What's going on?"

"Sorry, Mom, I meant to tell you last night but you were so tired. I want to stay in Lost Trail and open my own accounting practice. I was hoping—Aunt Marsha thought for sure you'd think it was okay—that Raven Farm could be my first client."

Rosemary swallowed, then sank onto a stool. "So you and Marsha have already talked about this?"

"Briefly last night." Tiff felt like the worst daughter in the world as tears filled her mother's eyes. "Mom. I thought you'd be happy."

"I want you here. Yes. It just hurts to find out second hand this way."

"Rosemary, don't be so sensitive. The topic just came up when we were watching TV together. It's not like Tiff planned to tell me before you. I've made a fresh pot of coffee. Let me pour you a cup."

"I suppose."

Tiff took a fortifying breath then sat down beside her mother. "I'd like to tell you what's been going on in my life the past six months, Mom. It might help you understand why I want to move back."

"Lost Trail is your home. This farm is your legacy. You

don't need excuses for living here."

"But there is stuff you need to know." And soon, before she found out Tiff had already told Marsha all this as well.

Quickly Tiff outlined the problems she'd been having with anxiety and insomnia, the mistakes she'd made at work, and her decision to lick her wounds while traveling after she was fired.

Her mom kept shaking her head. Every now and then she bemoaned the fact that Tiff had waited so long to tell her any of this.

It was a relief when Rosemary decided to take her coffee upstairs to her room. Tiff felt the familiar burden of guilt as she watched her mother leave the room. She wished she could understand why conversations with her aunt were always so much easier than those with her own mother.

"Try not worry about your mom. She'll feel better after she has her coffee and a little quiet time."

Quiet time was the last thing Tiff thought her mother needed. Before all the tragedies Rosemary had been a regular volunteer at the library, as well as a great mom to her and Casey and a help to her husband on the farm. It would be so nice to see her engaged with her family and community again. Gardening and baking were active, at least, but they were also solitary endeavors that enabled her mom to continue living in a protected bubble.

Aunt Marsha meant well, but it seemed as if she was enabling her mom's isolation rather than helping her overcome it. The last thing Tiff wanted was to criticize the woman who had done so much for her family, however, now that Tiff was here to stay she was going to make it her own private project to try to draw her mom out, little by little.

"What kind of sandwiches should I make?"

"I was thinking chicken salad. If you're okay doing the sandwiches yourself, I'll run upstairs to shower and change."

"Sure, I'll be glad to." She found cold chicken breast in the fridge, which she mixed with chopped celery, chives, apples, and walnuts. Then she blended in some mayo and a little curry powder.

She had a plate of sandwiches prepared when she heard a tap at the back door. Kenny stood at the other side of the French doors, dressed in his customary jeans and plaid jacket. His dark hair was unkempt and the scruff of beard on his face looked longer than usual. There was a wild look about the man that should have been off-putting.

Annoyed with herself—because she wasn't put off, not even a bit—she waved for him to come inside. He did so, removing his boots and leaving them on the mat by the door.

"Hey, Tiff. I'm here to meet with your aunt."

"I've heard. In fact, I'm going to sit in."

"Oh really? That's great I guess."

Hearing the reservation in his voice, Tiff gave him a fake smile as she carried the plate of sandwiches to the table.

"It's a family business, and I am part of the family."

"So I report to you, as well as Marsha. Got it."

"That's not what I meant. If you should be reporting to anyone other than Marsha it would be my mother. She's the legal owner."

"Yeah. But in name only, right? Since I started, I've only dealt with Marsha. She's the one who hired me." A corner of his mouth turned up in a half smile. "Though, maybe that's a decision you'd like to revisit?"

"Should I?" she countered. "Aren't you doing a good job?"

"I am," he said with quiet confidence, before adding, "At least, until this thing with Riley, I thought I was."

Tiff heard the caring in his voice and saw it in his troubled brown eyes. "Why do you say that? You can't feel responsible for what happened to her—do you?"

"Strictly speaking, no. But she was so young and as her boss I should have looked out for her more than I did."

"If you shoulder a degree of responsibility, so should my family. We were her employers."

Marsha appeared then and the subject was dropped. Kenny produced a sheaf of paper that included a rough monthly cash flow. While they munched on sandwiches they discussed orders, and the timing of deliveries that all needed to take place by mid-November. After that they would focus on local holiday business. Over ninety percent of profits came from the out-of-town orders, but the local business was important too. For over four decades families in Bitterroot

County had been coming to Raven Farm for their Christmas trees. Tiff was glad to see that Kenny understood this tradition was important to the family, even if the profits weren't particularly significant.

Once they'd finished with the financials and Marsha had signed the weekly checks, Marsha asked how the workers were doing in the aftermath of Riley's death.

Kenny rubbed a hand over his jaw, and his gaze met Tiff's briefly, in silent acknowledgment of their earlier conversation. "The guys are shaken up," he said finally. "Hell, so am I. I…feel like I failed that kid somehow."

"Riley told you herself she came here hoping to make a fresh start," Marsha pointed out. "Obviously she was running away from trouble. Even the sheriff suspects someone from her past did this to her. You shouldn't feel guilty. All you did was try to give her a second chance."

Kenny nodded, but his troubled expression remained. Tiff wanted to believe it was genuine concern for Riley, but what if it was more than that? Could Kenny be concealing information about the woman or her death—maybe because it was something he felt would make him look bad?

Tiff didn't know him well enough to tell.

Marsha held up the coffee pot. When Tiff shook her head and so did Kenny, Marsha refilled her own cup. "Moving on to the reason Tiff is sitting in on this meeting…" She paused to smile at Tiff. "My niece is going to be starting up an accounting practice in Lost Trail."

"So you're staying this time?"

His tone struck Tiff as both cocky and condescending. "I am."

"Her mother and I are so glad. We want her first client to be Raven Farm."

Kenny leaned back in his chair, his expression suddenly distant. "What does that entail, exactly?"

"I'll do the bookkeeping, tax returns, payroll."

"Leaving you to focus on operating the farm and managing the workers," Marsha continued. "We won't be adjusting your salary if that's worrying you."

Kenny glanced from Marsha to Tiff. As he rubbed his face, Tiff noticed a muscle ticking madly at the corner of his jaw. Finally he let out a long breath. "Can't say I love paperwork, anyway."

"Good." Marsha smiled as she got to her feet. "Kenny, you might as well show Tiff around the office now. Let her get her feet wet."

"No problem," Kenny said.

But from his cool tone and stiff posture, Tiff suspected the opposite.

THE FARM OFFICE in the far corner of the barn was another place where time seemed to have stood still after Tiff's father's death, showing no permanent mark of Ed's years as manager. When Tiff and her brother were kids, behind the sofa had been one of their favorite spots for hide-and-seek. Tiff had also loved playing with the adding machine, which still had a place of honor on the scarred surface of the old fir desk.

The office smelled the same as it always had—a combination of clean sawdust and the sharp perfume of evergreen resin. Tiff had tried to find an aromatherapy oil that could compare with the scent of balsams and pines…but nothing in a bottle could match the real thing.

She took a deep breath and smiled, almost forgetting about Kenny until he sat in the brown leather office chair behind the desk.

Was this his way of telling her, she might be taking over the accounting, but he was still boss of the farm? Fine with her.

She could sense Kenny watching as she wandered the room, checking the old photos hanging above the sofa where her dad had sometimes grabbed a quick afternoon nap. The photos dated back to the early nineteen hundreds, documenting the history of the farm from the first field of planted conifers, to the latest barn renovation.

Tiff moved to the bank of black metal filing cabinets on the wall perpendicular to the desk. They were old and dented, but still functional. She slid one open and saw legal files, carefully labeled, most in her father's scrawling hand.

It was all so very familiar. Too familiar in fact.

She turned to study the desk. There was the old phone, one with a cord and a rotary dial for heaven's sake! The glass jar she'd painted in kindergarten still held a motley selection of pens and pencils. But—

"Where is the computer?" She couldn't see a modem either. "We do have Internet out here, don't we?"

"I can usually catch a few bars from your home Internet. As for a computer, there wasn't one when I arrived. I use my own laptop." He nodded at a slim notebook on the corner of the desk. "But not for accounting. That's still done the old-fashioned manual way."

"With ledgers?" She'd learned the theory in college but had never worked with them in a real business situation.

"Yup." Kenny pointed to a line of oversized, leather-covered books on the shelves behind the desk.

"Wow. Unbelievable."

"I guess neither your dad nor Ed was a fan of computers."

"I'm not surprised to hear that. But my first order of business will be to buy a new computer. It's not right that you're using your own for farm business. Then I'll convert the manual accounts to a nice, simple farm accounting software. I'll have to do some research before I pick one."

"You mean you didn't have any farming clients in Seattle?"

She acknowledged his dry sarcasm with the faintest of smiles. "Hard to believe, right?"

Glancing back at the desk she noticed something else that was new—a framed photograph Kenny must have brought with him. Four men in backcountry ski gear were lined up on a snow-covered mountain ridge. The sharpness of the focus, the brilliance of the blue sky backdrop, made it hard to look away.

"Is one of these you?"

"Second from the left. The lead guide that day was Rolph Werner." Kenny pointed to the older man beside him, at the end of the line. "That guy taught me everything I know about backcountry skiing. He had all the skills and knowledge, but also a sixth sense about the weather and the mountains."

She noted the past tense. "Did something happen to him?"

Kenny looked like he was sorry he'd said anything. "He was guiding a group in Glacier National Park, on a day when the avalanche risk was less than moderate. He'd gone ahead to check a slope that looked a little suspicious to him. I guess he had a sixth sense about it, even though he'd done some slab tests and it all looked good. For once the fates were against him."

"He triggered an avalanche?"

Kenny nodded. "He was seventy-one and he'd spent his life skiing in the mountains he loved. He was a fearless man, but never reckless. What would have mattered most to him was that none of his clients were injured."

The man was obviously a hero to Kenny. Yet Tiff wondered if Kenny also felt some envy. Rolph Werner had lived until his seventies doing a job he loved, yet here was Kenny, barely thirty by the looks of him, already sidelined from skiing by a knee injury.

"Do you think you'll ever get back to guiding?"

"Not likely, even once I've had surgery—which I can't afford right now—I won't be able to do hard-core stuff like that."

"But you'll still get the surgery...eventually?"

"That's the plan." He got to his feet after checking the time. "I've got to go back in the field. You'll let me know if you need anything from me? Accounting-wise?"

There'd been the tiniest of pauses between his two questions, as if he worried she might want something that wasn't related to accounting.

As if.

"Sure. I'll see if I can get a computer this weekend, then start diving into the actual work on Monday."

Kenny shrugged, basically reminding her that this accounting gig was her and Marsha's idea, not his.

Tiff took a last look around the office, absentmindedly straightening a cushion on the ancient sofa. A flash of pink caught her eye and she moved the cushion out of the way.

"What the hell?" Kenny strode forward, snatching the pink bit of cloth and throwing it in the garbage, but not before Tiff saw what it was.

A pair of women's silky, pink thongs.

Chapter Fourteen

ZAK WAS REVIEWING crime scene photos when Nadine came in, letting out a showy sigh to communicate her exhaustion.

She dropped her jacket and holster on her desk, then picked up her mug. "Any coffee left?"

The buttons of her regulation shirt strained over her breasts. Sure, she wore a T-shirt underneath, but couldn't she size-up and give guys like him a break?

He turned his attention back to his computer. "Just the dregs from the afternoon pot. I would have made more but it's almost six."

"After I inventoried the items in Riley's car, I took a look around the parking lot and found traces of blood on the gravel beside the car. It seems whoever hit her did it there, then dumped her off at the medi-clinic."

"That fits with Dr. Pittman's preliminary report. He figured she'd been moved after the attack. Did you find anything helpful in the car?"

"Would have loved to find an address book or something, but no such luck. All I saw was clothing, a notebook and pen, some books, a sleeping bag and pillow, a paper bag with a few homemade cookies, empty cola cans, and a stack of napkins from Lolo's Pizza. I took photos for the files."

"Anything interesting in the notebook?"

"It was filled with sketches, most of them of a house, from various angles, with detailed drawings of each room. She was pretty talented."

"Did you recognize the house? Was it someplace here in Lost Trail?"

"I don't think so. I'm guessing she was designing her own dream house—"

A dream house she would never live to see, thanks to the brutal actions of someone—but who? Zak didn't believe this had been random violence. But what had caused the rage in the man—or possibly very strong woman—who had done this?

Nadine cleared her throat, drawing his attention back to her. She folded her arms and looked at him pointedly. "Interesting that you told me exactly where to look for that car."

If she'd pressed the issue, he would have filled her in. But since she didn't, he let the question hang.

"So where are the sheriff and Butterfield?" she asked.

"They went to the Dew Drop half an hour ago. They should still be there if you hurry."

"How about you?"

"I'll be heading there shortly too."

"Meeting your friend Tiff again?"

"As it happens—yes." Tiff had phoned a few hours ago and said she needed to talk to him. He'd been glad to hear from her. He was worried the sheriff wasn't going about this investigation as thoroughly as he ought to be, and Zak needed a sounding board.

"Sure you're just friends?"

"Last I checked."

Nadine made a face at him, then sat down at her desk. "Maybe I'll type up my reports before I go. Other than finding Riley's car, though, I didn't have much luck. I must have covered half the town, but I can't find anyone who saw her after she left work on Halloween. Surely she wasn't just sitting in her car from six until two in the morning."

"Did you try the Dew Drop?"

"The staff there didn't recognize her photo. Patsy Larkin at the Snowdrift Café says Riley was a regular, but the last time she saw her was Monday morning when she came in for a muffin before heading to work."

There weren't many other places in Lost Trail she could have hung out. "Lolo's Pizza?"

"She was a regular there, too, but she always ordered takeaway." Nadine started typing on her keyboard, but after just a few minutes she paused. "Any interesting developments here today?"

"Sheriff spent most of the day on the phone with California. He's lined up a Detective Bowering to check in with the Blake family and interview the staff at the bar where Riley used to work."

"And Butterfield?"

"Not sure what he was doing, but he managed to make the job last all day."

"It's a true gift that man has."

Zak grinned. It was nice that at least one of his co-workers had a sense of humor.

"So what's up for your weekend? You and Tiff going to catch a movie in Hamilton?"

Why was she so insistent on making the two of them sound like a couple? "I'll go for my usual run on Sunday. Not much else planned."

"You're a runner. That explains why you're so skinny."

Yes. Thank you, Nadine—just the comment every guy wants to hear.

"So what's your distance?"

"On weekends I like to get in thirteen miles or so."

Up went her eyebrows. "A half marathon. Impressive. Want some company for the first five miles—that's my limit?"

"I don't mean to be rude, but I prefer to run on my own."

She stared at him for a moment. "Maybe you don't mean to be rude, but actually, you just were."

His face grew hot. Damn. She was right. "I haven't had a running buddy since high school, that's all. If you're serious, meet me at the beginning of Tamarack Trail at eight."

"Tamarack Trail…" She raised her eyebrows. "So that's how you knew."

✕

TIFF HAD A pitcher of draft and two glasses on the table when Zak arrived at the Dew Drop at about quarter past six.

"Sorry I'm late again."

"No problem. I'm guessing you've had a busy day. Maybe I should have ordered bourbon?"

Tiff had her hair down tonight, which was hands-down her best look. He could never understand why she seemed to prefer ponytails.

For some reason her eyes always looked bluer when her hair was down. And her features prettier.

He noticed a few guys in the room had their eyes on her. Why was it, in all the years they'd been friends, he'd never felt the urge to try and take their relationship beyond the platonic? He flashbacked to the way Nadine filled out her regulation shirt and felt like groaning. He did not want to complicate his life by having a crush—or worse an affair—with a co-worker.

"Maybe we'll get to bourbon after this." He had his first, long swallow of beer, then sighed with satisfaction.

"I told my family about my plans to stay in town and start my own business. Mom and Aunt Marsha seem cool with the idea."

"Of course they are."

"And they've agreed to let me handle the accounting for Raven Farm."

"Did you seriously worry they wouldn't?" Ready to order some food, he tried to catch Mari's eye, but she walked right by him. "How does Kenny feel about it? I assume you'll be taking the work over from him."

"He kept his face deadpan, but I had the sense he was annoyed. Plus, get this, Zak. When I went with him to the farm's office, I spotted a pair of women's pink underwear under one of the sofa cushions."

"Hang on a minute. There's a sofa in the office?"

"Yes. I didn't get as far as the office when I gave you the tour, but my dad was known for enjoying a fifteen-minute nap in the afternoon. He hated having to walk all the way to the house, so when Mom renovated the living room, she had the old sofa moved to Dad's office."

Zak nodded. Her explanation had given him time to process the significance of the pink panties. "Riley was the only female employee at Raven Farm, right?"

"Yes," Tiff answered emphatically.

"Is it possible Zak was entertaining a girlfriend in his office?"

"I can't see that happening. The guest cabin where he's living is much more comfortable and romantic. Not to mention private."

"The underwear couldn't possibly belong to your aunt or your mother?"

Tiff cringed. "Ew. No. These panties were so tiny, just thongs. As soon as he spotted them Kenny grabbed them and pushed them into the trash."

"Did he say anything?"

"No. And I didn't dare ask about them. He looked absolutely furious." Tiff waved a hand at Mari who was hurrying by them again. "Two burgers please—with fries. Sound good, Zak?"

"Sure. No onions on mine though," he added with little hope since Mari had already turned away. Too many burgers and fried foods wouldn't be good for his running regime…let alone the alcohol. But after the week he'd just had, Zak felt entitled.

Tiff leaned in closer, lowering her voice. "Here's the thing. If Kenny was sleeping with Riley, why didn't he tell the sheriff?"

"One pair of underwear doesn't prove anything, Tiff."

"If the DNA on the panties was a match, it would, right?"

"Well, we'd have to get a search warrant and we don't have enough evidence for that."

"You need a search warrant. I don't. It's my home, after all. But guess what—I went back to the office an hour later with a plastic bag and the trash can was empty. Why would Kenny have eliminated the evidence if he had nothing to hide?"

"Hm." It did sound suspicious.

"Whenever Kenny talks about Riley he refers to her as a kid. I wonder if he's trying to deflect any suspicion that they might have had an intimate relationship." Her eyes widened as another idea occurred to her. "Do you think Riley might have been charging Kenny to have sex with her?"

Zak thought back to Justin's visit to the sheriff's office that morning, how keen he'd been to get his visit from Riley documented, under his terms. Two different men, both having spent time alone with Riley—a woman who had basically admitted to having an unsavory past.

"Given what happened to her, we should probably consider the possibility. It certainly sets up the scenario for her death." He couldn't tell Tiff about Justin's statement, unfortunately, but he could string along the logic. "If Riley was trying to earn some money on the side, it stands to reason she might have arranged to meet a man the night she was killed."

"My aunt was talking to Dr. Pittman at work yesterday. He as good as assured her that Riley hadn't had sex the night she died. I suppose the transaction could have gone off the rails before they got to that part."

"We need more evidence." He took a deep breath, then leaned in closer. "But I don't think the sheriff is open to any theory other than his own. And he's keen to pin the crime on someone from Riley's past, someone with no ties to Bitterroot County."

✕

TIFF STUDIED ZAK'S face. She trusted her friend, and his instincts. "I remember my aunt saying once that nothing short of an unsolved crime spree could ever prevent Archie Ford from getting re-elected as county sheriff. I can see how it would look better for him if he could prove someone outside the county killed Riley. But would he really put his own self-interest ahead of justice in a murder investigation?"

"In a case where he wasn't worried the perp would re-offend? He might."

Tiff nodded. "What about his deputies?"

"Butterfield takes all his cues from the sheriff. The new deputy, Nadine Black, is sharp. But she's pretty new to be challenging the sheriff."

"Then I guess it's up to you to make sure Riley gets her justice."

Before Zak could respond, Mari arrived with their order, and the aroma of grilled meat and smoky seasonings was completely distracting.

When in South America Tiff had eaten mostly chicken and legumes for her protein. At the time she hadn't felt deprived. But now that she was home, all she wanted was the Montana beef she'd been raised on. Barbecued tenderloin was her favorite. But the burgers at the Dew Drop—spicy and juicy, served on fresh sesame buns with homemade sauce and caramelized onions—were a close second.

She'd enjoyed two big bites before she noticed Zak pulling out the onions again.

"You should try them. They're delicious."

He looked at her as if she'd suggested he suck on slugs.

"Whatever. It's your loss." Tiff scooped up his rejected onions and made room for them on her burger. As she took another bite, she scanned the room. The sheriff, Deputy Butterfield, and Dr. Pittman had been sitting in the far corner on the other side of the room when Tiff had arrived. She'd purposefully sat as far from them as possible, so Zak wouldn't feel as if his superiors were monitoring him on his off-time. Now they were gone, the sheriff and deputy home to their wives and children, Dr. Pittman home to what must be his cavernous house on Lost Creek Road.

Their table was now occupied by a young couple out on a date. The way they were leaning in toward one another, things were going well.

There were lots of ranch hands in the bar also. A few of them had dates, but the single guys were mostly gathered around the bar. At another table for two against the wall she spotted a familiar-looking older couple. It took a few seconds for her to recognize Derick's parents, Will and Jen Sparks. They each had a highball glass in front of them and were picking away at a plate of nachos, though neither looked to be enjoying them much.

"Wow, Derick's dad looks so much older since I last saw him."

Zak followed her gaze. "He hasn't been the same since his heart attack. Lucky for him he's been able to hand over most of his business responsibilities to Derick."

"Jen is as gorgeous as ever." As a teenager Tiff had been in awe of Derick's mother. She'd always dressed nicer than anyone else in town, and even in her own home, she was never without makeup or nicely styled hair.

"She works at it. She's in Missoula twice a month for her beauty appointment and every February she takes a three-week trip to an exclusive beauty spa in Arizona. I imagine she'd look a little older without those."

"Ah, small towns. It's so much fun knowing everyone's dirty secrets. Too bad they get to know yours in return." It wouldn't be long before everyone heard she'd been dumped by her boyfriend and fired from her job. Oh, well. Now that she'd told Marsha and her mother, neither one felt quite as tragic as they had six months ago.

"The key is not to have secrets."

She studied Zak's open face. Did he think she had no idea what had been going on behind closed doors in the Waller household? She decided not to challenge him.

"I wonder how Will and Jen feel about being grandparents."

"Will seems like the kind of guy who would care about having an heir. Someone to inherit the business, you know?"

Zak asked.

"Ugh. I'd hate to grow up with those sorts of expectations." Never once had her father or her mother implied she or her brother would have any responsibility toward Raven Farm when they grew up. She would have railed against the idea back then.

Now she found herself wondering about her mother's will for the first time in her life. She had no siblings or cousins. If she didn't want the farm, she supposed it would be sold after her mother died.

The thought of that made her sadder than she'd thought it would.

Tiff took a closer look at the older couple's expressions. "I wonder what they're doing here? Neither one looks very happy. You'd think they'd rather be spending time with their new grandson."

"They always come to the Dew Drop on Friday night. I guess they're creatures of habit."

"By the way, I tried to visit Derick and Aubrey yesterday. I even had a gift for the new baby. But they claimed the baby was sleeping and didn't even invite me in."

Zak stabbed his fork at his French fries until he snagged one. "That's weird. I don't get Derick these days. It's like he's turned into a different person."

Tiff considered that last sentence. Zak had a point, Derick had changed. "I'm not sure I should say anything, but I noticed a faint bruise on Aubrey's face. She claimed she walked into a door when she was up late with the baby. You don't think Derick could have—?"

Zak stared at her. "The old Derick—no way."

"I agree. He was a killer on the football field, but in real life he was always so gentle and unassuming. His parents leaned on him hard about his marks. Most kids would have been angry or resentful, but he took their criticism in stride. I can't remember him ever losing his temper."

"Me either," Zak admitted. "But maybe the stress of taking over the family business and being a new father is getting to him."

Chapter Fifteen

S ATURDAY ZAK CLEANED his apartment, started a load of laundry, and then drove in to Hamilton to pick up groceries and run a few errands. When he'd been a kid Lost Trail had not only his dad's hardware store, but also a bank and a Super 8 grocery. Back then the businesses had been supported by a population that was at least double what it was now. Many locals worried about Lost Trail shrinking. It seemed most of the younger generation left as soon as they finished school. But as long as he had a job with the sheriff's office, Zak was more than happy to stay.

On his way home from Hamilton, Tiff called to suggest they meet up at the Dew Drop again.

"Not tonight," he told her. "I've had my quota of beer and burgers for the week." The extra calories would be detrimental to his running, but they weren't his real reason for declining. Nadine's teasing was getting to him. He liked hanging out with Tiff, but Saturday night was for couples.

So Zak spent the night making notes about the homicide case, with Watson on the sofa beside him pretending not to care, but occasionally batting the pen with a fast swipe of his paw. Zak knew the sheriff would not appreciate his insights. But Tiff was right, Riley deserved justice and if he could figure out what had happened to her he might be able to guide the others in the right direction.

Though, if he was honest with himself, he had to admit getting justice for Riley wasn't his sole motivation. The truth was, he'd always loved a good mystery. He cared about the young woman who'd lost her life so tragically, but intellectually he was drawn to the puzzle as well.

He wouldn't make the mistake of discounting the possibility that the sheriff was correct. Top of the list of motives had to be an unresolved problem from Riley's past. Maybe she'd stolen some money from that ex-boyfriend of hers. Or seen something she shouldn't have.

Also on the list though, should be the possibility she'd angered someone in Lost Trail. Perhaps a john, assuming she'd started her own escort service. Which she might have done out of a desire to save money for that dream house she'd been sketching.

Somehow neither of those theories meshed with his brief impression of Riley. She'd dressed more like a street urchin than a hooker. And she'd seemed genuinely embarrassed to be caught out sleeping in her car. She hadn't given him any attitude at all.

Yet there had to be some reason she'd been out so late the night she was murdered...

Finally Zak dropped off to sleep, and for the first time

since his family left town his dreams were dark and foreboding, juxtaposing scenes of a menacing call girl swearing at him from the corner of a street that did not exist in Lost Trail, with others of Aubrey, crying and imploring him to run for help.

It was a relief to get out of bed at six, even though it was still dark. Zak made himself a green power smoothie and used his computer to catch up on international news. Dull light was seeping from the eastern horizon when he finally headed for the park, walking briskly as a warm-up for his run.

Did he expect to find Nadine waiting for him? Not really, but there she was, geared up in leggings with a black and white geometric pattern, neon green running shoes, a bright pink jacket, and her blonde ponytail pulled through a white hat.

"Colorful."

"It is hunting season."

"Not in a state park." He pointed out the signage.

She shrugged. "This was the warmest stuff I own for running. It's freakin' freezing out this morning."

"Well, it is November. Ready?" He started at a slower pace than normal, picking his way along the needle-strewn dirt path. The trail followed the river for the first few miles, before veering off in long, gentle switchbacks up the flank of Strawberry Peak.

After five minutes he realized Nadine was matching him

stride for stride and he increased the pace. She kept up, no problem, with breath left over for talking.

"You missed a wild time at the Dew Drop last night. You and Tiff go to the movies after all?"

He ignored the question. "What happened?"

"A couple of ranch hands felt they were both entitled to dance with the same girl. I had to give them my drunk and disorderly talk."

"Any violence?"

"A few punches. But once I flashed my badge they calmed considerably. So what movie did you see?"

He checked his Garmin. They were doing a good pace. Maybe if he went faster he could shut her up, but he'd risk sabotaging his own run too.

"I stayed in last night. Did some thinking about the Concurran case."

"You think a lot for a dispatcher."

"I see things. Hear things. Can't help coming up with some ideas."

"Anything you'd like to share?"

"I've been speculating about the years between Riley moving out of her friend's house in San Francisco and her turning up in Lost Trail."

"Far as we can tell she was living on the street during that time."

"No family, no fixed address, no real way to support herself. So what might some women do to support themselves in those circumstances?"

Nadine snagged a toe on a root, then hopped to regain her balance. He paused, waiting for her.

"You're suggesting she was a prostitute?"

Her ability to keep a conversation going while she ran at his pace was impressive…and a little annoying. Zak had expected to be able to run her into the ground.

"What do you think?"

"It's possible," she conceded. "The boyfriend Emily Blake thought was a bad influence—"

"Connor."

"Right, Connor. He could have been her pimp as well."

"Exactly. So she runs away from him, finds this innocuous job in Lost Trail, and once she's established, figures she can earn some extra money on the side. Only—bonus—no pimp to share the money with."

"Any evidence to support this theory of yours?"

"Only circumstantial." He wouldn't share his hunch about Justin, but he did tell Nadine about the underwear Tiff had seen in Kenny's office. "If they were having consensual sex, why would Kenny lie about it? Sure she was his employee and that's not cool. But Riley was murdered, he has to know better than to lie when the sheriff comes around investigating."

"I see what you mean. If he paid for the sex he'd be a lot more reluctant to admit it. But there's also the possibility the panties belonged to another woman—perhaps a girlfriend of

Kenny's."

"But in that case, wouldn't he take her to his cabin? They'd have more privacy there, not to mention a lot more comfort."

"You're right. Having sex on the sofa in your office implies acting on impulse."

Zak tried to block the image of him and Nadine, alone in the office on Friday night…No. He shouldn't go there. Not even in his imagination.

He brought his wayward thoughts back to the present and checked the running stats on his watch. Two miles down, and Nadine was still going strong.

He resumed discussion of the case. "If Riley was prostituting herself that would also explain why she met someone so late that night. Maybe it was a john."

"And something went wrong before they got down and dirty. Yeah." Nadine gave him a sharp look. "That's good thinking. You should tell the sheriff your theory Monday morning."

"If you think it has any merit, go ahead and bring it up."

"What the hell? You don't want credit?"

"The sheriff would take the idea more seriously if it came from you."

Nadine started to slow down. He paused to see if anything was the matter. "I thought you wanted to go for five miles?"

"Turns out this is enough." She bent over at her waist

and rested her hands on her thighs. After a few deep breaths, she stood tall again. "You don't make any sense, Zak Waller." Then without giving him a chance to say anything else, she took off running back toward the parking lot.

✕

ZAK WAS STRETCHING his quads after his run when he noticed a woman in a blue parka with the hood up, carrying a baby in a sling-like contraption next to her chest. She was heading for the trail he'd just finished and almost passed right by him before he recognized her.

"Aubrey?"

She started. Blinked at him. "Oh, hi, Zak. Did you have a good run?"

"Pretty good." He brushed his sleeve across his sweaty forehead. Before she'd gotten engaged to Derick, he'd had a bit of a crush on Aubrey. Just his luck she'd see him at the end of his run instead of the beginning. Sure she was married now. But a guy had his pride.

"Congratulations on your son. Brody, right?"

She shifted the blanket shielding the baby's face from the cold. "He was screaming up a storm when we left, but he's sleeping now."

Zak took a peek. "Cute."

Aubrey gave a weary smile. "Yes. When he's sleeping. Which isn't as often as the books say."

"He's a rule breaker is he?"

The baby squirmed, and his mouth puckered as if he'd tasted something sour. Aubrey began to sway. "I have to keep moving or he'll wake up. Want to walk with us a while?"

Now that he'd stopped running, his body was chilling rapidly. But he couldn't bring himself to say no. "When did you and Derick bring Brody home?"

"Hard to believe, but it's been almost two months now."

"Has it been a difficult adjustment?"

"It's changed everything, but in a good way. I'm thrilled to be a mom. I hadn't counted on Derick being such an anxious father, though. He's so worried about exposing Brody to germs he doesn't even like visitors coming to the house. I had to practically beg him to let me go on a walk this morning."

When she twisted her face to look at him, he could see the bruise on her temple. He studied her eyes, looking for signs of this happiness she was talking about.

The wetness pooling in her eyes was not reassuring.

"Derick's folks must be excited to be grandparents."

"They love the idea of a grandchild. But not when it's crying or has a poopy diaper. That's fine though. Derick and I have it covered."

"What about your parents?"

She ducked her chin, but not before he saw her lower lip tremble. "I was hoping my mom would come and stay for a while. But she only does Montana in the summer now."

Aubrey kicked a pine cone off the path. "That's her excuse. The truth is my new step-dad isn't happy unless he has her undivided attention."

"That's tough. But I'm sure you and Derick are doing a great job on your own."

"Thanks, Zak. I needed to hear that." She paused to glance at her watch. "Darn, I'd better turn back. Derick didn't want me gone too long."

Zak was so cold he had to work hard not to shiver. But he would have kept going if she wanted. As they reversed directions she said, "I've been so rude, monopolizing the conversation. How are things with you?"

"Work's been busy. Obviously."

Aubrey's eyes widened. "I forgot you're working at the sheriff's office. Of course you've been busy. That was awful what happened to that poor woman."

"Yes. The sheriff is anxious to see the bastard behind bars as soon as possible." Especially if the bastard was from another county—preferably another state—from his own.

They were back in the parking lot now and since their routes home both required them to turn onto Driftwood Lane, Zak figured they'd walk together for a few more blocks, but Aubrey unexpectedly turned left.

"I have…a little errand to run before I go home. It was nice to see you, Zak."

She was gone so quickly he didn't have a chance to ask her about the bruise.

✕

JUSTIN SPENT SUNDAY afternoon preparing a roast beef dinner. His father was coming over at six and he wanted everything to be perfect, the way his father had made it for him when he was growing up.

"So these Sunday dinners are going to be regular things?" Willow was setting the table while he peeled potatoes. Geneva was on the floor piecing together a jigsaw puzzle Justin had purchased for her when he'd been in Hamilton for a meeting on Friday.

"Do you mind?"

"It just feels so traditional…Sunday dinner with the family. Sometimes I feel like I've stepped back in time since I moved here."

He was sure the years she'd spent traveling with Paul had been nothing like this.

"Can you handle the change? I think it will be good for Geneva."

"You're probably right. And your dad looks like he needs the calories. Does he eat properly, I wonder? He's so much smaller and thinner than I remember."

"He was never a very big man." Unlike his son. As a teenager, Justin remembered his dad always preparing lots of food. But had he kept up the habit after Justin moved out? Probably not. "Next time I visit him I'll check his fridge. I wouldn't be surprised if he isn't taking time to cook for himself."

"He's lucky to have such a caring son."

"It's only fair, given what a good dad he was to me." It did worry Justin, though, how much he meant to his father. It was why he hadn't confided the truth about his cancer—he'd been afraid of his dad worrying too much. Luckily the side effects from the chemo hadn't been too harsh. He'd been able to explain away his thinness with some vague references to new food allergies, and his thinning hair he'd concealed by shaving off his hair.

If this new mass turned out to be cancerous, though, his oncologist would likely suggest a bone marrow transplant. Justin would need to come clean about his health then, with both his dad and Willow.

"Do you remember what your dad was like before your mother died?" Willow was looking at the wedding photo of his parents he kept on the mantel. "He looks so young and happy here."

"I was only six, but I do remember. Mom's death really changed him."

"And he's never even dated anyone since then?"

"Not that I know of. When I was younger I liked it being just the two of us. I hate to admit to being so selfish, but I probably would have resented a new woman in his life. Now nothing would make me happier than to see him find someone."

"If he hasn't in all these years, I doubt he will now. Some

people still do mate for life in this world, hard as it is to believe."

It was a romantic notion and from Willow's wistful expression, Justin suspected she was thinking of Paul. An ugly jealousy surged briefly, painfully, in his chest, proving he hadn't managed to put the past behind him as successfully as he'd hoped.

His father's signature five raps sounded on the front door then. It was exactly six o'clock and his punctual father had come bearing gifts. A bottle of wine for dinner and a plastic crate containing the old train set Justin had loved as a child.

Standing slightly behind her mother, Geneva's gaze was riveted on the crate.

"This Thomas the Tank Engine train set is pretty hard to put together. Would you be willing to give me a hand, Geneva?" Clark placed the crate on the floor and let the little girl peer inside.

Solemnly she nodded.

"Thanks for the wine, Clark," Willow said. "Can I pour you a glass?"

"Maybe later. Geneva and I have some train building to do."

Justin watched his father get down on his hands and knees. He let Geneva pull out the pieces, one by one, not hurrying her, or showing her how the pieces fit together, unless she asked.

"He's so good with her." Willow returned from decanting the wine, and handed him a glass.

"Yeah. He was like that with me, too."

"The potatoes are ready. Want me to mash them?"

"Sure. I'll come make the gravy."

As they worked together in the kitchen, the murmur of his father's voice from the living room filled Justin with a sense of rightness. Contentment. This was what it meant to be a family. His father clearly loved being a grandfather. Justin glanced at Willow, his earlier jealousy forgotten as his heart expanded with gratitude that she had made all this possible for them.

"I wish I could get Geneva to connect with me as well as she does with my dad."

"Don't take it personally." Willow paused, seeming to consider something, before adding, "Paul is a tall guy like you and he could be emotionally volatile at times. I think Geneva is a bit on edge around you, in case you ever act the way he did."

Justin's heart contracted abruptly, painfully. "Did he ever hurt her?"

"No." Willow let out a long breath. "At least I don't think so."

What? He forced himself to count silently, *one, two, three.* When he trusted himself to be calm he turned to her. "Tell me the truth, Willow."

"I'm not sure what the truth is. Paul was impatient with Geneva and I didn't leave them alone together often. But when I took Geneva to the clinic last month to catch up on her vaccinations for the day care, the nurse said a few things that worried me."

"Such as?"

Willow kept her gaze on the pot of potatoes, even though she'd stopped mashing them. "She commented that Geneva was quiet and withdrawn compared to other children her age. She asked about developmental milestones…had Geneva been slower than other children in walking, talking, being potty trained…"

"And? Was she?"

"It's hard to say. Children learn to do these things within a fairly wide range of ages. But as I thought about it I realized Geneva had always been in the slower zone of each range. Especially in potty training."

"But she goes to the bathroom fine now. So what's the issue if she took a little longer than normal?"

"Probably nothing. But the nurse's probing didn't feel casual and when I got home I did some web surfing. Her questions were the same ones medical professionals ask when they suspect something is wrong at home…"

Willow stopped there, but she didn't need to say more.

Justin felt as if his throat had suddenly swollen to twice its normal size. "No," he managed to say. "Paul wouldn't."

"That's what I've been telling myself."

Their gazes connected, and Justin saw the same thing in hers that he felt in his own heart.

Insidious and corroding.

Doubt.

Chapter Sixteen

O N MONDAY MORNING the sky was an icy blue and the grass crunched with frost as Tiff headed for the barn, laden with the new purchases she'd made during a trip to Missoula that weekend. Halfway there she was joined by Spade who had been sleeping on the sunny front porch of the guest cottage.

"Hey, old boy. Want to help me set up a new accounting system today?"

Spade panted agreeably.

Though four trucks—presumably belonging to the hired help—were angle-parked by the barn, no one was around. The guys must already be out working in the fields. Spade's pace picked up as Tiff made her way inside. As soon as Tiff nudged open the office door, Spade rushed inside. He circled the room, carefully sniffing out the corners, then settled on a rag rug next to the desk.

Spade had come to the family a few years after her father died. He'd been her dog for years, sleeping in her room and following her around whenever she wasn't in school. But after she'd left for college, he'd been a little lost. Now that she was back, she wondered if she could convince her mother and aunt to let him live in the main house again. Maybe if she offered to clean up all his accidents?

Tiff set down the box containing the printer onto the floor, then shrugged off her backpack where she'd stowed the new laptop. The office looked as if it had been freshly cleaned and the only items on the desk were the phone, the adding machine, and the jar of pens. Kenny had removed the framed ski photograph.

Tiff checked the garbage next—still empty—then the sofa. The cushions looked freshly plumped, but she couldn't stop herself from checking behind them.

Nothing. Of course there was nothing. Kenny would have made darn sure of that.

Finally she could procrastinate no longer. She plugged in the laptop. She'd never converted a manual accounting system before. Hopefully it wouldn't be too complicated.

As she settled into the old leather chair she realized this was probably the same chair her father had used, back when he was running the farm. What would he say if he could see her here now? It wasn't hard to picture him coming into the room, looking surprised and then pleased.

Though he'd been gone for twenty years, Tiff thought of him often. Playing the "what if" game probably wasn't healthy, but she couldn't seem to stop herself from wondering what her life would have been like if he'd lived.

Better yet, if her dad *and* Casey had lived…

The computer was asking her to set up a password. She typed in *RavenLunatic.*

Which was what she would be if she didn't start focusing on the present rather than the past. But even as she went through the steps of setting up a new email account for the farm—she couldn't believe they didn't have one, yet, let alone a website—her thoughts began to drift again, this time to yesterday, when she'd gone to church with her mom and Aunt Marsha.

After the service, they'd visited with their friends and neighbors while sharing coffee and sandwiches in the church basement. Her aunt had quickly been swallowed into the crowd, while Tiff had made a point to stick close to her mom. She'd been shocked to see how her mom's old friends patronized her. Only Sybil had bothered to have a real conversation with her mom, not seeming to mind the vague responses Rosemary gave her.

At first Tiff had been overcome with her usual anger. She'd wanted to say, *Come on, Mom. Snap out of it already, would you?* But slowly compassion had overtaken the anger and she'd realized that getting her mother to re-engage with the world was going to be more difficult than she'd thought. A good start might be to get a second medical opinion. Hopefully her aunt and Dr. Pittman wouldn't take it as an insult.

Eventually the intellectual challenge of setting up a new chart of accounts pushed Tiff's worries to the back of her mind. She became so engrossed she worked through lunch and was surprised when her aunt showed up with a sandwich and some cookies.

"I figured you must be hungry. Egg salad okay?"

"Sounds yummy. I'm starving." She saved her work, then set aside the laptop to make room for the plastic containers. "Thanks, Aunt Marsha, but you didn't need to go to all this effort. At some point my hunger pangs would have forced me to take a break."

"I don't mind having the chance to fuss over you now and then." Her aunt flipped a few pages in the Accounts Payable Ledger sitting on the corner of the desk. "So how is it going?"

"I'm easing into it. Once I've set up the chart of accounts I'll start inputting opening balances, and eventually create a link to our bank account. Going forward every transaction will automatically get recorded in our books."

"I would say that sounds awesome except I don't under-stand half of what you just said."

Tiff laughed. "Basically the bookkeeping is going to be a lot easier once I've finished the setup."

"Well that's wonderful." Marsha ran a hand along the bookshelf, straightening one book, then adjusting a mug from the National Christmas Tree Association. "Have you started looking for other accounting clients yet?"

"No. I wanted to get up to speed here first." Tiff had a feeling her aunt was going somewhere with this. "Do you think I'll have trouble finding more work?"

"It's possible. Lost Trail is a dying town. Every few years it seems we lose another business. I'm afraid you'll invest your time and money in this venture only to realize you can't make a go of it."

"If that happens maybe I'll let Kenny go and start running the farm."

She'd been joking—sort of—but her aunt's appalled expression surprised her.

"Would that be such a bad thing for me to do?"

"Personally, I'd love it. But your mom was talking to me this morning, and while she'd never admit it to you, she's worried about your decision to live in Lost Trail."

"Really?" Tiff tried not to sound hurt. She'd always assumed—incorrectly, apparently—that the option of running Raven Farm would be open to her if she chose it.

"She's afraid your talents will be lost in this small town. But her bigger concern is letting you down. At church today, you were trying to be kind by sticking so closely to her, but she felt you were trying to push her into interactions she would have preferred to avoid."

"But—we were just talking to people she's known her entire life."

"Simply attending church is difficult enough for your mother. She's happiest living a simple life, here at home."

"But is that really happiness? Cutting yourself off from your community and all your friends?"

"I don't believe your mom has wanted to be happy since your brother and father died. She just tries to carry on."

"Is it possible she's suffering from an undiagnosed medical problem?"

"Clark and I have done our best to find medical solutions, but heartbreak isn't always treatable. Now, don't go bringing up this subject with your mother. It will only upset her needlessly."

"Right." Tiff put down her half-eaten sandwich.

Once her aunt returned to the house, she tried to focus on the accounts again, but worry for her mother kept distracting her. She went to the window and looked out at the view down the valley. Row upon row of noble fir stretched across the hill. On the other side of the gentle valley she could see the Scotch pine—her personal favorite when it came to Christmas trees.

The usual time span to grow a tree to maturity was about ten years—which meant the last trees planted by her dad had been harvested about a decade ago.

So many years. Was it really his death and her brother's that were responsible for her mother's mental state? Shouldn't she be showing at least a little improvement after so much time?

Aunt Marsha seemed to think every medical avenue had been explored. But she was going to broach the idea of getting that second opinion with Dr. Pittman.

WITH SPADE FOR company, Tiff went for a long walk, to clear her head, careful to avoid the field where the men were harvesting. She didn't want to make small talk, or deal with Kenny and the complicated way she felt when she was around him.

As she tromped through rows of fragrant fir she noticed threatening clouds mounting from the north. Given the bite in the air she guessed a snowstorm was coming. It wasn't yet winter, but in Montana snow rarely waited for an official invitation.

Last night she'd pulled up YouTube video clips of Kenny's various skiing adventures. There were lots of them. The more she investigated, the more she appreciated his strength and skill. From accompanying comments and links to various blogs and magazine articles she could see he had a respected name in the industry and was one of Montana's highest-rated backcountry ski guides.

The fall that had resulted in his sprained knee had been caught on camera and was spectacular. Watching him fly off the cliff, tumble in the air, then awkwardly hit the ground on one leg before smacking into a tree, she couldn't believe he'd survived.

His injuries, besides the sprained knee, had included a severe concussion, several cracked ribs, and a dislocated shoulder.

Something else she'd learned from the Internet was that before his accident Kenny had been engaged to Kate Novak from the Canadian National Olympic ski jumping team. There was a clip showing Kenny watching on the sidelines while Kate competed in Sochi. Then another of the two of them carving powder in Glacier National Park.

There were no videos, blog comments, or articles about a break-up, but Tiff guessed one had occurred. The only question was whether Kenny or Kate had been the one to pull the plug.

As she looped back toward the barn Tiff became aware of the grumpy engine sounds of a big tractor. A moment later the John Deere came into view, pulling a trailer loaded with fir.

She hurried her pace, hoping to make it inside before the driver noticed her, but she was too late. The engine quietened with a shudder, and then Kenny jumped to the ground. At that moment Spade left Tiff's side and loped toward Kenny, tail wagging enthusiastically.

Kenny bent to pat the dog, then headed for the barn, holding the door open for her. "How's the bookkeeping going?"

He smelled of sawdust and pine resin, familiar aromas that for once did not give her a sense of comfort. His cheeks were reddened from the cold, and his scruff of a beard had a hint of frost on the bristles. As always his deep-set dark eyes were inscrutable to her.

"Fine. I just needed to clear my head." She had a hard time meeting his gaze, unable to stop herself from picturing him in a compromising situation with young Riley.

"Finding everything you need?"

"Yes." She stepped back from him a bit. "I noticed you cleaned the office."

Their gazes met and this time they held. She waited for him to say something about the pink underwear. Surely he had some explanation to offer.

"What you saw the other day…I wouldn't want you to get the wrong impression."

Right. She bet he didn't. "But that underwear—it did belong to Riley?"

He cleared his throat. "Yes—but it wasn't what it may have looked like. I would never—"

When he paused, she raised her eyebrows.

"Hell, don't make me spell it out."

Despite the theory she and Zak had discussed last night she wanted to believe him.

He shook his head. "I shouldn't have brought it up again. I was just hoping to clear the air. Seems I got off on the wrong foot with you from the beginning. You didn't like finding me in the cabin and you didn't like me helping myself to a mug in your family kitchen either. I assure you, I'm not trying to butt in on your territory."

She wanted to deny all the pettiness he was accusing her of. But it was true. And it was unwarranted. She had to offer him some sort of explanation without admitting that the real reason she felt uncomfortable around him was a lot more complicated.

"My life in Seattle blew up this year. When I came home, I was hoping for some peace and stability."

"And a new farm manager was too much for you?" His tone was mocking, but not unkind.

"This isn't just about you."

It was about her mom getting worse rather than better. And Derick, so friendly on Facebook but now avoiding her. And, of course, the murder of Riley Concurran. Since her brother's and father's deaths Tiff had been all too aware that life could deliver some wicked blows. But the brutal murder of a young woman, an employee of Raven Farm, was unfathomable.

"We have to work together, Tiff. It would be nice if we could get along."

"I can't argue with your reasoning."

"Why don't you come over for a drink later tonight?"

Her mouth went dry. This wasn't a proposition, was it? "You mean to the cabin?"

He shrugged. "It's where I keep my alcohol."

Nothing in his expression or tone suggested an ulterior motive for his invitation. "I guess one drink wouldn't hurt. What time?"

"Whenever. Like you and your mom, I'm a night hawk."

How did he know…?

"I go for drives some nights when I'm feeling restless, and I see lights in the upstairs windows. Used to be just the room over the garage. Now there are two lights burning late. You and your mom always had trouble sleeping at night?"

"Not always. No." His gaze was piercing, and she had an atypical urge to reveal more, which she resisted. "Let's say around nine. I'll bring the bourbon."

DINNER THAT NIGHT was a solitary affair for Tiff. Her aunt had a book club meeting in town and her mother decided to have a simple soup and sandwich up in her room. It seemed meals in her room where not unusual for her mom.

Tiff ate her own soup and sandwich in front of the TV watching the local news. Lost Trail's homicide was the leading story, and included a short interview with Sheriff Ford who spoke reassuringly about the victim's questionable background in her home state of California and how authorities there were checking into the whereabouts of her former boyfriend.

How clean and tidy. Tiff wondered if Zak was watching and what he thought of the sheriff's take on things. Personally, her stomach ached whenever she thought about the young woman who had worked on Raven Farm only to end up dead in a back alley in Lost Trail. Maybe the culprit was someone from another state, a part of Riley's earlier life.

But until the evidence of that was found, Tiff thought Zak was right to consider other possibilities.

At seven Tiff went to her mother's room and found her sleeping, her meal only half eaten. She stood quietly for a few moments, gazing at her mother's delicate features. When she was younger Rosemary had been known for her glowing, clear skin. But time was taking its toll. There were faint wrinkles at the corners of her eyes and puckered skin along her upper lip. From the deep frown grooves on her brow, it seemed, even in sleep, she found no peace.

Back in the family room Tiff read for a while, then at nine, grabbed a bottle from the liquor cabinet, put on her coat and boots, and went out the back door.

At some point while she was inside it had started to snow and now a full two-inch coating lay on the ground. The flakes were falling so slowly some of them seemed to be floating in space. No wind rustled the branches of the fir trees. All was silent except for the crunch of her boots through the snow as she made her way to the cabin, guided by the bluish light from the moon.

She knocked at the wooden door and heard Kenny call out, "Come in." A second later Spade let out a lazy bark, as if he knew it was her at the door and was barking as a matter of obligation.

She stepped inside quickly, squatting to give the old family dog a hug. Spade wriggled appreciatively.

The guest cabin on Raven Farm was basically one large

room with an attached bathroom. The open space was divided by furniture groupings into three areas: a kitchenette, a bedroom with a queen-sized bed, and a sitting area where a leather sofa faced the fieldstone fireplace.

Tonight the only light came from the glow of that fire and two table lamps on either side of the sofa. The atmosphere might have been romantic except for the sound of a football game.

Kenny was in the kitchen area, taking a tray of ice cubes from the mini fridge. He'd obviously showered recently. His curly dark hair gleamed with moisture and the air felt humid, redolent with a fresh, crisp soapy smell.

He grabbed the remote and muted the volume on the game. "Hey there. Still snowing outside?"

Instead of answering, she shook the snowflakes from her hair, then slipped off her boots and draped her coat over a chair. Her eyes were adjusting to the dim light and everywhere she looked she could see signs of Kenny's occupancy.

The bistro table held his laptop and a large ceramic mug she didn't recognize. An assortment of books, magazines, and a pair of gray and red striped woolen socks were on the low table in front of the sofa, and the fireplace mantel held several unfamiliar framed photographs, including the one he'd previously kept in the farm's office.

Kicking off his socks seemed to be a habit with him. There were socks under the kitchen table as well as beside his bed—which had been made in a very lazy manner, pillows askew and feather duvet lumpy.

She brought the bourbon to the kitchen where he had set out two tumblers.

Kenny nodded his thanks. "Want me to add some ice, ginger beer, and a little lime? My version of a Dark and Stormy."

"It's the perfect night for it." Except it wasn't really. When the hard blizzards of winter rolled off the mountains and down from the Arctic they usually came with blustering winds, driving snow, and chilling cold. Tonight's weather front was delivering the snow softly, as if anxious not to shock the world as it transitioned toward the upcoming cold, dark season.

She watched as Kenny mixed the drinks, noting the callouses on the tips of his long, elegant fingers.

"Was it hard adjusting from ski guiding to working on a farm?"

"I like the routine here better than I thought I would. Both jobs are physically demanding, but in different ways. I'm glad I get to spend the majority of my time outdoors."

"What does your family think of the change in your career?"

"We're not close. I don't let their opinions concern me much." He passed her a glass, then raised his in salute. "Cheers."

He'd shut that avenue of conversation down pretty fast. Not too sure what to talk about next, Tiff went to check the other photos on the mantel. They were all shots from his skiing days, one she recognized from a magazine article in *Backcountry* she'd found online.

"What do you think of the drink?"

She went to take a sip, but the sharp tang of ginger made her cough. Holding her breath, she tried a second time. The bourbon, ginger beer, and lime went down smooth and spicy. "That's good."

He came to join her by the fireplace, standing close enough that his arm brushed against her shoulder. She inched to her left. "Looks like some epic ski trips."

He pointed to each photo in turn naming the state and the mountain. "Some of my favorite places in the world."

"So it's the places, not the people, you want to remember?"

"A little of both."

"I googled you," she admitted. "You have quite a reputation as a ski guide. I also saw your name linked to an Olympic ski jumper from Canada. Kate Novak."

"You've really done your homework. Did you run a security check too?"

"Should I have?"

"Your aunt phoned my references before she hired me. Maybe you could rely on that. As for Kate, yes we were engaged, but after my accident I needed some alone time. Once I was strong enough, I drove the West Coast highway. Ashamed to say I got into some trouble in the bars I stopped at along the way. Then I got beaten up badly one night and that helped set me straight. I went back to Kate and told her I needed to change my life completely. Settle down, maybe start a family. Kate wasn't on board with that, so we parted. Amicably."

She swept a sideways glance over his face, trying to gauge his level of heartbreak.

"I missed her at first. But I'm doing fine now." He raised his eyebrows at her. "How about you?"

He'd been open with her, it was her turn now. She tried to give an honest answer. "I'm getting there."

"So what did happen out in Seattle? To hear your mom and aunt talk you were living a charmed life, getting promoted every third year and had a boyfriend who treated you like gold."

"It's a long story."

"We've got time. And a lot of bourbon left in that bottle. Want to sit down?"

She glanced at the sofa. Sitting made sense. And yet, something about that sofa, which wasn't especially long, felt too intimate. So she perched on the rock ledge of the fireplace, right next to old Spade who was curled up to take best advantage of the warmth from the fire.

Kenny went to the sofa, laying his arm along the back and angling his body so he occupied more than half the space.

"My life was going along really well," Tiff admitted. "But

last winter, I started falling apart. I can't say why. I started having anxiety attacks at night when I was trying to sleep. I'd end up staying awake until dawn, then falling asleep and getting to work late."

"And this hadn't happened to you before?"

"Never. I was always an early to bed, early to rise kind of person. Drove my friends crazy in college. But it served me well at work."

"Until the anxiety attacks."

"Yes. Not only was I getting to work late, I was also exhausted. I started making mistakes. Little ones at first. Then I messed up an important set of financial statements and compounded my error by arriving at the audit committee meeting a full hour late."

"Sounds bad. But not unforgivable."

"I haven't told you the worst part." She dug her fingers into Spade's thick, brown coat. The dear old dog turned and gave her hand a lick, before dropping back to sleep. "The reason I slept in on that occasion was because I'd gone home for the night with the client's son."

"Oh. Not so cool."

Unable to meet his gaze, she glanced into the fire. She'd already said too much, but she found herself continuing. "No, it wasn't cool. Especially since I had a boyfriend at the time. We'd been together for years. Everyone expected we'd be getting married soon, including me. Needless to say, that will never happen now."

"The boyfriend found out?"

"I told him. How could I not? Anyway, I lost my job and my boyfriend and so I decided the logical next step would be to go traveling until I'd blown all my savings." She forced a smile. "So there's my story."

Kenny said nothing for a long while. Finally she glanced at him, and was surprised to see a total lack of judgment in his eyes.

"Want some more bourbon?"

She hadn't realized her glass was empty. "Another Dark and Stormy? Sure."

He took their glasses back to the kitchen area.

The drinks were strong and a second probably wasn't a good idea, but it felt good being in this cabin with Kenny. She was beginning to forget why it was she'd taken such a strong dislike to him at first. When he returned with the refills, she was sitting on the other side of the sofa.

"Decided I won't bite?"

She smiled. Truth was, she wouldn't mind if he did. She held her breath and took a sip of the fresh drink. "Even better than the first one."

"Well, go easy this time, Tiff. These drinks are strong."

They'd covered his past and hers. Tiff moved to the next obvious subject of conversation. "Did you listen to the news tonight? It sounds like the authorities in California are on the hunt for Riley's ex-boyfriend. Did she ever talk about him with you?"

"No. She didn't discuss her past, period. She was quiet. And I thought a little sad, too. It was part of why I felt sorry for her."

An image of the silky pink thongs came back to her. Kenny had assured her the situation wasn't as it appeared. But suddenly she remembered something else. Her mother telling her that the night Riley died she'd thought she'd heard a vehicle in the driveway. Her mother had gone to the window and seen no one—but maybe that was because the vehicle hadn't been arriving, but departing.

Kenny, going to meet Riley?

Hadn't he just told her today he sometimes went for a drive when he couldn't sleep? Maybe he'd been trying to create a cover story for himself.

Fear pressed a cold hand to the back of her neck despite her immediate rationalizations. Maybe her mother had imagined the sound. It could have been someone other than Kenny. Logic told her both explanations were perfectly plausible.

Regardless, she no longer felt safe here with him. She set down her glass abruptly. "You're right. These things are too strong for me. I'd better go home. Check on my mother."

Kenny looked taken aback, but he didn't argue. At the door, he offered her the bottle. "Not much left, but you should take this with you."

"That's fine." She didn't dare meet his gaze in case he saw too much in hers. "You keep it."

Outside the snow was still falling. She could hardly see her own footprints from earlier. She started out walking but then she ran. Tonight she would be locking all the doors and windows.

Chapter Seventeen

J USTIN CREPT FROM the bathroom to his bed in the dark, sliding between the sheets carefully so he wouldn't wake Willow.

"It's okay," she said softly. "I'm not asleep."

"Sorry. I tried to be quiet in the shower." After tucking Geneva into bed, he'd spent two hours working out in his downstairs gym. He'd needed to push himself physically to keep his dark thoughts at bay. His hope had been to exhaust himself so he'd fall asleep quickly.

"I was having trouble sleeping anyway." She was quiet for a moment then said in a tone he rarely heard from her, one that was almost beseeching, "Will you hold me?"

"Of course." He moved closer, adjusting his body to accommodate hers. After their marriage he'd started wearing cotton T-shirts and boxers to bed. She snuggled her face against his chest.

"You always smell so nice."

"I didn't twenty minutes ago."

She traced her hand down his chest to his six-pack. "No wonder you're so buff. You work out a lot."

"It's a good release for me. But maybe I should ease off on my workouts. Spend more time with you?"

"Oh, I'm fine. I took a few books out of the library yesterday. Geneva and I both got new library cards. I'd forgotten how nice Sybil Tombe is. She invited us to the preschool reading circle on Thursday."

"Good idea. Geneva can meet some kids her age. But do you think Geneva will go?" Since her move to Lost Trail, the little girl had been reluctant to try new things or meet new people. His dad was pretty much the only person she appeared to enjoy spending time with.

"I think so. Sybil was good at drawing her out. She let Geneva play with the hand puppets they use for story hour. Geneva seemed enthralled."

"Might be good for you, as well. Maybe you'll like some of the other parents."

"Maybe."

She sounded skeptical and he didn't push. A few weeks after Willow and Geneva moved in with him, he'd suggested inviting some of their old school friends over for dinner. Willow vetoed the idea.

"When we were growing up you were pretty much the only person in Lost Trail who didn't bore me to tears. I came back to be with you. No one else."

"And I appreciate that. But you'll go stir-crazy if you don't get out and meet people. Do things."

"I'll sort out the problem of what to do with my time on

my own. Just don't expect me to fall into whatever mold married mothers fit in this town. I'll only disappoint you."

"Be yourself. Do whatever makes you happy, and I'll be good with that."

The words had been easy to say back then, before she'd turned herself into a virtual hermit. Once a week she drove with Geneva to Hamilton to do grocery shopping and other errands, but the only other time he'd heard of her venturing downtown had been to take Geneva to the clinic for her vaccinations.

"It's snowing tonight," Justin said, brushing his fingers over her dark, silky hair. "But it's supposed to be sunny in the morning. Maybe you guys could go for a walk…and take your camera. I bet it'll be gorgeous out."

As long as he'd known her, which had been since kindergarten, Willow had been obsessed with photography. As a little girl she'd carried around a boxy green camera, made for children, but as soon as she was old enough to babysit, she'd saved up money to buy her first Olympus.

When she'd moved in, he'd seen she now owned top-of-the-line professional equipment, including an array of lenses and a tripod. He'd offered to renovate half the basement for her, set it up as her own photography studio.

But she'd shaken her head and stowed the equipment away in a large plastic tub.

"You forget, I've lived here before. I've taken every sort of picture you could imagine in Lost Trail."

"None with Geneva, though."

"Photographing people isn't really my thing."

He felt her stiffen in his arms. She hated when he pushed her, but he couldn't help himself. Willow's boredom was practically palpable. She desperately needed to find something stimulating to occupy her time. She was too much of a free spirit, too creative and adventurous, to be happy as a stay-at-home mom in a town that bored her.

"You know what Geneva told me after I read her bed-time story?"

"Hm?" Willow lifted her head.

"She said her other daddy thought you were the most talented and beautiful woman in the world."

"Really? She said that?"

"Yes."

"Amazing. Paul did used to say that all the time. I think she got it word-for-word."

"Well, Paul was right. You are talented. And beautiful."

"Please," she protested. "Paul can get away with that sort of hyperbole. But truth is more your style. I have made some beautiful pictures, I agree. But only because Paul took me to some of the most stunning places in the world."

Despite his effort not to react, he could feel his body tense.

"I don't mean to complain," she added hastily. "Traveling with Paul was fun while it lasted, but what we have here with you is much better for Geneva. And that means a lot to me. So thank you." She kissed him softly on the cheek.

He noticed she said nothing about what was better for her. "I still have a way to go with Geneva. I think she's starting to trust me. But as hard as I try, I can't seem to build the same rapport with her that my father has."

"I still think it's your size. Your father is a smaller man. Less…threatening."

Now they were brushing up to the topic that had been in his thoughts since their conversation last night. He couldn't resist probing again.

"Do you think Paul could have abused her?"

"I've told you, no. He wouldn't. And yet—ever since that nurse made those comments I've been going over things in my mind. I told you Paul didn't have much patience with Geneva. He sometimes spoke very harshly. And I did see him swat her once. He swore it was the first time and he'd never do it again…but what if he did? Maybe I loved Paul and the lifestyle he provided so much, I subconsciously ignored signs that should have sent me packing a lot sooner."

The familiar ache of jealousy as she talked about her love for Paul paled in comparison with his concern for Geneva. "Paul was usually so charming and amusing. But he had a cruel side."

"Yes."

Willow kissed his cheek again, then turned over and burrowed into the covers on her side of the bed. "Good night, Justin."

"Love you." He stared up at the ceiling waiting for the deep, slow breathing that would tell him she'd fallen asleep. It didn't happen for the longest time.

Chapter Eighteen

ZAK WAS TRYING to make sense of the notes the sheriff had just dropped on his desk when the phone rang at two-thirty on Tuesday afternoon. Seeing the name on the call display he didn't want to answer. But of course, he had to.

"Bitterroot Sheriff's Department."

"Is that you, Zak Waller?" Cora Christensen was using the same tone she'd scolded him with when she'd been his teacher. "I need to speak to the sheriff."

"I'm sorry but Sheriff Ford isn't available right now." This was the truth. The sheriff was in his office with the door closed, on the phone with that detective from California. But Zak would have said the same thing had the sheriff been standing in front of him, twiddling his thumbs. Part of Zak's job—a big part of it—was shielding the sheriff from calls like this one.

"I've been very patient. I realize the sheriff has that awful murder to investigate. But you would think in the week since I phoned in to report the vandalism of my dining room window, *someone* might have found time to get my statement and take photographs."

"I'm very sorry. You're right, though, we have been extremely busy." He'd thought Nadine had been going to handle this last week. He tried waving at her to get her attention, but she was focused on her computer, as invisible to him as she'd been since her Monday morning conversation with the sheriff.

She'd made several rookie mistakes when she'd raised the theory that Riley might have started turning tricks in Lost Trail and been killed by one of her johns.

First, she'd started talking before the sheriff had his coffee.

Second, she hadn't made it sound like this idea had emerged from something the sheriff had said or done.

And third, she'd assumed the sheriff would want her to follow up right away and so she'd already done some preliminary legwork.

Zak had watched the sheriff's eyes grow smaller and smaller the longer Nadine talked. Zak had tried to give her a hand signal to stop, but either she hadn't seen it, or she hadn't appreciated how annoyed the sheriff was getting.

Finally when she'd finished laying out the case, much as Zak had done with her during their run on Sunday, Sheriff Ford had given her a dismissive smile.

"Interesting theory. But I think I'd know if this woman had been turning tricks on the main street of my town. We need to focus on the California angle. Figure out who that ex-boyfriend of hers was and find him. Check for his DNA on the victim's clothing, and once we have a match, all we'll need is a pretty pink bow before we send this case to the state prosecutor."

Nadine had stared at him, dumbfounded. At which point the sheriff had practically patted her on the head.

"You're new here. Young and eager. It might take a while to get the feel for how we do things in this county."

Since then Nadine had neither looked at nor spoken to Zak, which wasn't fair since Zak had warned her the sheriff would not be receptive to the theory.

Then again, life was not fair. And in Zak's experience, that was especially true where he and women—of all ages— were concerned.

"Last week I could have washed my window but I was afraid to disturb the evidence. Now the weather has turned and all the egg has frozen on the glass. I'm not sure I'll be able to have clean windows again until spring."

"Someone from the department will come today, Miss Christensen." Since Butterfield was out patrolling, it would have to be Nadine.

"I certainly hope so, Zak Waller, or I'm going to be very disappointed in you."

Duly noted. "Thanks for calling, Miss Christensen."

He hung up before she could add a parting insult, at which point Nadine finally glanced up at him. Before either of them could say anything, the sheriff burst out of his office.

"Where's Butterfield?"

"Still on patrol." And if Zak knew the deputy, he wouldn't be checking in again until morning.

"Do you have that list of items that were in Riley's car? Butterfield was supposed to send that to Detective Bowering yesterday."

"I have the list as well as photos." Dr. Pittman had already gone through it carefully looking for evidence of prescriptions or drugs that might shed a light on Riley's medical history. "Should I email it to the detective?"

"Yes!" the sheriff barked.

"Will do." Zak shuffled papers to find the record of a call that had come in right before Cora Christensen's. "Gertie Humphrey phoned in at one-fifty. Claimed a strange man filled up at the Conoco pumps this afternoon. She said he was a tall man, dressed in fancy jeans and expensive shoes. Not from around here. Car was a rental from Budget."

"How old was the guy?"

"She thought early thirties."

"She get the tag on the vehicle?"

"She's pretty sure about the first four numbers."

"Could be the boyfriend, though I would expect he'd be long gone by now." The sheriff turned to Nadine. "Go check with Keith at the Dew Drop. Find out if he's had any out-of-towners check in this week and, if so, get any details he's willing to share."

Nadine's voice was cold when she said, "You want that

done now, Sheriff? I'm still working on locating Riley's ex-boyfriend, following up leads from Jack's Cellar."

"Yes, I want it done now. You can get back to this—" he waved a hand at her computer "—when you've got my answers for me."

It didn't take Nadine long to slip on her holster and her jacket and exit the office. On her way out the door she gave Zak the briefest, iciest of looks, before shutting the door with considerably more force than necessary.

The sheriff shook his head slowly.

"Should have known better than to hire a woman. Right, Zak?"

Zak raised his eyebrows expressively. He'd have to warn Nadine. She was going to need to modify her style—a lot—if she wanted to keep this job.

WHEN ZAK LEFT the office at six-thirty that evening, Nadine was back at her desk, on her phone. Each conversation seemed to add a bunch more names to her list but none of them so far were named Connor. She'd learned nothing significant from Keith at the Dew Drop either. The few registered guests he'd had this week had been folks in town to visit relatives. Her frustration was obviously growing with each passing minute.

He guessed he wasn't going to be popular when he reminded her about Cora Christensen, but to his surprise, she merely nodded.

"Yeah. I've put that off too long. Where does she live again?"

"I'm on my way home. Follow me and I'll point out her house."

She looked surprised at the offer, but nodded.

Zak drove to the edge of town, parking across the street by the graveyard. Hard to believe only a week had gone by since he'd found Tiff Masterson paying her respects to her brother's and father's graves. A hell of a lot had happened in that week.

The walkway up to Cora Christensen's house was covered in snow. While Nadine was inside getting the old lady's statement, Zak pulled the shovel he kept for emergencies from his truck and cleared off the path.

Much as he'd hated the old biddy when she was his teacher, he couldn't help feeling sorry for her now. From what he could tell she lived a pretty lonely life. When he was done he took a gallon of windshield wiper fluid from his truck and tried to wash the egg off her window. He'd gotten most of it clean when the front door opened and Nadine stepped out.

"Thank you for the cookie," Nadine said. "Can you show me where you saw the boys?"

A sweater-covered arm poked out through the open door, pointing at a spot across the street in the graveyard.

"That's where they were hiding. Thirteen years old, I'd guess. Fourteen at the most. When I opened the door to give them a piece of my mind, one of them started throwing the eggs. I think he was aiming for me, but missed and hit the window. Then the boys took off at a run."

"Did you recognize them?" Zak asked.

Cora poked her head around the door. "Is that you Zak Waller?"

"Yes, ma'am."

She glanced from the gleaming window pane back to him. "There was a time when I knew every boy in this town. But I've been retired for sixteen years. Of course I can't tell you who they are. Isn't it your job to figure that out?"

He decided it wouldn't be prudent to remind her he was just a dispatcher.

"And did you notice the time when this happened?" Nadine asked.

"It was almost three in the morning! What sort of parents let their children roam around the streets at that hour?"

The question was obviously rhetorical so Nadine merely nodded. "Right. I'll be sure to relay everything you've told me to the sheriff."

"I'd appreciate that." The old lady stepped out onto the landing to get a closer look at her window. "You left a streak, Zak Waller."

Zak supposed this was what he got for trying to be kind to the old biddy. With a flourish he wiped off the last of the egg. When he glanced back at the door, it was closed. Only Nadine stood on the landing now and she was laughing.

"What a good sport you are."

"Obviously she liked *you*. Did she actually offer you a cookie?"

"Yes, but I didn't dare eat it." Nadine took a grayish-looking oatmeal cookie from her pocket. "I think it must be five years old, at least." She crumbled it into pieces and tossed it into some bushes. "Maybe the birds will like it."

Zak tossed the half-empty container of wiper fluid back in his truck. "So what did you think of her?"

"Weird. Her house looks so tidy and pretty on the outside. But it's a mess inside. Piles of boxes, and papers, and plastic bags. I swear she's a hoarder."

"That's nicer than anything I have to say about her."

Nadine glanced back at the house, just as the curtain in the front window twitched. "This is some strange town you live in."

"Tell me about it."

Chapter Nineteen

AS TIFF TURNED onto Winding Down Way she was surprised to see Zak's truck parked beside Miss Christensen's house. He'd been about to pull onto the road, but once he spotted her SUV, he stopped and got out of the cab. She left her vehicle, too, and met him on the cemetery side of the street.

"What are you doing here?" she asked.

"Nadine—Deputy Black—and I were just getting Cora Christensen's statement regarding some vandalism that took place here on Halloween night."

She glanced at the windows. "Window looks clean now."

"Yup. I cleaned it off for her. Did she thank me?"

"I'm guessing no. You're such a softy, Zak." Not many people would do such a kindness for someone they disliked.

"Either I'm soft, or I'm a fool. Possibly I'm both."

"Definitely not a fool." She glanced at the graveyard. "Though maybe I am. I get so frustrated at my mom for letting the past paralyze her, but I can't forget either."

"Coming home after being away for so many years was bound to make it all fresh in your mind again."

God, she was lucky to have a friend like Zak. "I have a few things to do in town. When I'm done do you want to meet at the Dew Drop? It's been a few days—I swear I'm in withdrawal."

"How about we meet at seven?" he suggested. "I'll go home and feed my cat first."

"Seven it is." She started for the path to the cemetery, then swiveled back. "You have a cat?"

"He sort of adopted me last year. We're on amicable, if not affectionate terms. I call him Watson."

Zak was just the sort of guy to offer a home to a stray, unwanted pet. She waited until he'd driven off, then went to check in on her brother's and father's grave markers. She ran her hands over the smooth granite and tried to let go of the old longing to have them back.

Twenty years was a long time. Why couldn't she let the past go? No one but her had ever thought her dad's accident was anything but that—an accident. As a kid, it had been hard to lose two of her most loved family members in just a few months. But she was an adult now, an adult who knew that sometimes bad things happened, and there wasn't always a reason.

Five minutes later Tiff drove to Tumbleweed Avenue and parked behind the medi-clinic. For a few seconds she lingered in her warm vehicle, staring at the rear entry. That was where they'd found Riley's body.

Had the killer been trying to get medical help at the clinic?

Or just looking for a quiet place to dump the body?

It felt creepy being here in the dark. No one else was around and only two vehicles were in the parking lot—her aunt's and the doctor's.

When she'd set out for town she'd hoped this would be the perfect opportunity to talk to Dr. Pittman about getting a second opinion for her mother. She didn't know what specialists her mom had seen over the years—she'd always left her mother's medical care to Aunt Marsha. But it was time for her to be more actively involved.

After a careful look around to make sure no one was lurking, Tiff made her way to the front entrance. Clinic hours had ended over half an hour ago, but the door was still unlocked. She went in through the foyer, stopping at the unmanned reception desk. To her right were eight wooden chairs, a water cooler, and a magazine rack. To her left was the corridor that led to the examining rooms.

She was just about to call out a greeting, when she heard a door open from within. And then her aunt's voice.

"You can't be serious, Clark. At this point it would be a disaster."

"I'm tired, Marsha. Sick and tired. I tell you, I won't do it anymore. I mean that."

Tiff froze. This sounded deeply personal. She couldn't let them know she was here. Quietly she retraced her steps to the foyer.

"You owe me, Clark."

It was the last thing Tiff heard before she slipped out the door.

TIFF TOOK HER time walking to the Dew Drop, trying to process the conversation she'd just overheard. The familiar way her aunt and Dr. Pittman had spoken to each other suggested there was a deeper—almost intimate—relationship going on between them. For some reason they'd kept it secret, and now there seemed to be a big issue between them.

Last thing she could do was ask her aunt. She'd overheard something that was none of her business. She had to do her best to put it out of her mind.

When she arrived, the Dew Drop was quiet. Only a few tables were filled, at one of them was Zak, scrolling on his phone as he waited for her.

As she slipped into the empty chair she resolved to keep quiet about what she'd just heard.

"I've ordered our beers and burgers," Zak told her.

"My mouth is already watering. I wonder how many days in a row I'd need to eat the Dew Drop burger before I got sick of it."

"For the sake of your health, I suggest you leave that question unanswered."

She glanced around, feeling her tension ebb away. The

owner, Keith Dewy, was behind the bar tonight, and his daughter Mari was once again waiting tables. She came toward their table now, with their beers.

"Thanks a bunch," Tiff said gratefully. Her first long swallow went down smoothly.

"You guys are becoming regulars," Mari replied. "Thanks for coming in on a Tuesday. It's typically one of our slowest nights."

"It's our pleasure," Tiff assured her.

"Your burgers are on the grill. They'll be out shortly."

As she turned toward the next table, Tiff said, "Remember to hold the onions on Zak's."

Mari nodded, then carried on.

"So we're Dew Drop regulars now," Zak said. "We have to be careful. People are going to talk."

He was right. "Would you mind if they did? I mean, have you got your sights on someone? I wouldn't want to mess up your chances if you did."

He hesitated a few seconds. "Nope. There's no one right now."

"I hate to be selfish, but I'm glad. You're my only real friend in Lost Trail. I don't know how I'd keep sane if I couldn't hang out with you." Especially since Derick was being such a hermit. She'd tried calling him again today and sending a message on Facebook as well. He hadn't replied to either.

"Hey, I'm glad you came home. You're a fresh voice of

sanity in a crazy world." Zak told her how the sheriff had refused to even consider their theory that Riley might have been selling her body on the streets of Lost Trail.

"What a moron. Listen to this. Last night Kenny invited me over for a drink and tried to convince me that despite the women's underwear I found in the farm office, it wasn't what it looked like. But I remembered something about my first night home, Zak. Mom told me on Halloween night she was woken around two-thirty. She thought it was a vehicle driving up to the house. But what if it wasn't someone driving in, but someone driving out? It's possible Kenny was heading into town to meet Riley. What time was she killed?"

"Dr. Pittman put time of death close to three a.m. So that would fit. Trouble is, can we prove it was Kenny's vehicle your mom heard?"

Tiff grimaced. "Unfortunately she didn't see anything."

Mari came then with their burgers, and the smoky, fresh-grilled smell made Tiff absolutely ravenous. Zak lifted the top of his hamburger bun and marveled. "They actually remembered to leave off the onions this time."

"I shouldn't have reminded her. I love getting your extras."

TIFF GOT HOME just after eight-thirty. Her aunt had started watching the third season of *The Fall*, with a fresh bowl of popcorn and some sparkling water with lemon on the coffee table in front of her.

"Want to watch with me? I can go back to the beginning of this episode."

Tiff studied her aunt's face, noting the dark circles under her eyes. It was so easy to take her aunt, and all she did for the family, for granted. "No, I think I'll check on Mom. How was your day at the clinic? You look tired."

"It was rather grueling. Fall influenza season is upon us I'm afraid."

Tiff hesitated. "And how is Dr. Pittman?"

"Oh, fine. He is loving being a grandfather to his son's new daughter. Geneva is all he ever talks about these days."

Was that a bit of jealousy in her aunt's voice? "That all happened so fast, didn't it? Willow coming back to town with her daughter, and then Justin marrying her and adopting the girl?"

"As you recall, Justin and Willow were inseparable when they were younger, so their getting married so quickly wasn't as rash as it might appear. But Geneva is a quiet, peculiar little child if you ask me. Reminds me of a lost chick who has fallen from the nest. Of course Clark has always been drawn to vulnerable people like that."

"What do you mean?"

"Oh his wife Franny was always a frail woman. He just doted on her, to an extreme, frankly. However, his caring nature is what makes him such a good doctor, so I guess I shouldn't complain, even if it does mean he sometimes takes capable, strong women like me for granted."

"Aunt Marsha, do you have feelings for Dr. Pittman?"

"What? *Romantic* feelings?" Her aunt's laugh sounded forced. "No, Tiff, that wasn't what I meant at all. There is no unrequited love between me and Clark."

Tiff smiled, but wasn't convinced. Her aunt and Clark had been disagreeing about *something* earlier this evening. The fact that it hadn't come up in this conversation told her Aunt Marsha was being far from open with her.

TIFF OFFERED TO read to her mother that evening and was surprised when her mother said yes, and again when she discovered she enjoyed it. Lately she was finding it easier to be kind to her mother, rather than judgmental and angry. Maybe it was a sign of her own maturity.

At ten o'clock her aunt came up with tea for Rosemary, as well as a sleeping pill. Tiff said good night to both of them then tried to do some reading in her own room.

After reading the same page over and over, she put the book down and turned out the light. She'd forgotten to close her curtains earlier, and now a stream of moonlight was falling directly on her pillow. She went to the window and gazed out at the front yard. A mean wind had started a few hours ago. Now it was rustling the fir trees and causing one long branch to rub against the metal roof.

She remembered when she was younger, how this house had felt like such a sanctuary to her. So much so that she'd found the sound of winter storms comforting. She hadn't even minded the occasional howling of coyotes until her father explained that they were probably the culprits behind the disappearance of their old barn cat Jasper.

With a pull of the curtains, she shut out the view, then, still feeling restless, wandered out to the hall. Lights were off in both her aunt's and her mother's rooms. She looked across the hall to her brother's old bedroom. Quietly she made her way to it, easing the door open and then slipping inside.

It was darker here on the west side of the house, but she didn't need to turn on the light to know the bed was still covered in the brown and green quilt that had been Casey's favorite. He'd been a hockey fan—the only time she could remember him complaining about his weak heart had been when their parents told him he could not sign up to play with all his friends—and the walls were covered with posters of all his favorites from the LA Kings, most prominently Wayne Gretzky.

The sound of the trees creaking and groaning was even louder in here. Tiff went to the window and peered out at the firs lined along this side of the house. They'd been planted at least twenty feet too close to the house, and had been heavily pruned, but her parents had never had the heart to have them cut down.

A dark shape moving beyond the trees caught her eye and Tiff tensed.

Someone was headed for the barn. Kenny? It was too dark and the distance too far to be certain, except for one fact. Who else could it be?

The figure disappeared behind a rise in the ground, and for several minutes after that Tiff saw nothing.

Then a faint light appeared from inside the barn. Slowly the light progressed through the building, finally stopping at a room in the back.

The office.

Tiff put a hand to her chest, she could feel her heart pounding fast and hard. It had to be Kenny and there wasn't one good reason for him to be prowling about the office at this time of night. She didn't feel brave enough to go confront him. Nor did she feel she could call out for help from her aunt or a neighbor. What would she accuse Kenny of…working late?

She stayed at the window for over twenty minutes, until finally the light went out in the barn and the dark form retraced his steps to the guest cottage.

Chapter Twenty

GENERALLY FOUR TIMES a year the matriarch of the Lazy S—at 88,000 acres, the largest ranch in Bitterroot County—came into town to modify her will. Justin never had forewarning of when these meetings would take place, since at ninety-one years of age Lacy Stillman did not make appointments. In her words, "How can I promise to be in a certain location at a certain time when I don't even know if I'll be waking up the next morning?"

Despite the hours of unnecessary work she caused him—most of which, in good conscience, he didn't bill—Justin enjoyed her visits and colorful conversation. Lacy Stillman had absolutely no filter and no compunction in sharing every detail of her life, and those of her married sons Eugene and Clayton, who each had their own ranch houses on the home quarter.

Wednesday morning brought Lacy into his office early, in fact when he arrived with key in hand at nine a.m., she was waiting on the street. A tiny woman, she was always decked out in the very finest of Western wear. Today she had a semiprecious gemstone-studded buckle on the belt holding up her Wranglers, as well as a beautifully embroidered Western-style shirt, a fitted sheepskin jacket, and dangling earrings of turquoise and red jasper to match her belt.

"What kind of lawyer starts his day at nine a.m.?" Lacy wanted to know as she followed him up the stairs with a spring to her step that belied her age by about three decades.

"A lot of them, I'd guess." On the landing, he stopped to unlock his door, then held it open for her to walk ahead.

"I've been up since five-thirty, young man. Had my toast and coffee and supervised the chores. I tell you, if I don't keep my eye on things, nothing gets done proper. Place will probably go to hell in a handbasket once I'm gone."

"Would you like another coffee, Lacy?" He turned on the machine in the corner and then refilled the water tank.

"I already had two cups at the Snowdrift, waiting for you to open. You go ahead and make one for yourself though. Eugene's wife has one of those fancy machines too. I guess cowboy coffee isn't good enough for her."

By cowboy coffee Lacy meant coffee boiled in water over a camp stove—or in Lacy's case, over her old-fashioned wood-burning stove. Justin had visited her ranch home, twenty miles from town, several times in the past and always felt like he was stepping back in time when he did so.

Lacy clung to tradition and the old cowboy way of life, while her sons Eugene and Clayton pushed for her to accept more modern and efficient ways of doing things.

Leaving the coffee machine to warm up, Justin ushered

Lacy to his office and pulled back a chair for her. "So how can I help you today?"

"You've got to fix my will. For years and years my boys have been begging me to buy these glorified golf carts for the ranch. They say they need them to get around the ranch quickly. I say, isn't that what our horses are for?"

"Horses need to be tacked up to get started, and groomed when the work is done. UTVs run with the turn of a key."

"Don't you start on me too, young man. Nothing beats a good quarter horse when it comes to ranch work. And we've got tractors for the heavy work. I've been really clear about that, but this weekend Eugene went out and bought two of those contraptions for the ranch. Spent over thirty thousand dollars!"

"In his defense, Lacy, most of the larger ranches use UTVs as well as horses these days."

"We have standards at the Lazy S. At least, as long as I'm alive we do." Her shoulders sagged a little. "Unfortunately Eugene figures we'll lose too much money if he takes them back, so we're stuck with them."

Justin waited for what he knew could come next.

"But I want you to take thirty thousand dollars off his share of my estate. He had no business spending that money without my consent."

"You're sure about that, Lacy?"

"Darn tooting."

"Okay, I'll draw up an amendment and bring it out for you to sign in a few days."

She gave a long sigh of relief. "Thank you, Justin. Those boys got to learn, when they don't listen there are consequences. Now, if you'll excuse me I have to go drop some puppies off at the animal shelter in Hamilton."

"Puppies?"

"That silly wife of Clayton's had to go buy a purebred border collie last year. Before she got her fixed, that collie went out socializing and ended up fraternizing with the neighbor's mutt. Net result? Four puppies, and while they're cute as hell, we can only keep one of them."

"How old are they?" He and Willow hadn't talked about pets. But a puppy might be just the thing to bring Geneva out of her shell.

"Twelve weeks. Justin Pittman, are you thinking of adopting one of them?"

Before he could answer, a wide smile bloomed over her sun-worn and wrinkled face. "You absolutely should take one of these pups. They'd be perfect for that little daughter of yours." Lacy pointed to the girl at the center of the family portrait he'd recently added to his bookshelf.

"No family is complete without a dog," Lacy added, her smile turning smug, as if she knew she'd already sealed the deal.

✕

JUSTIN MEANT TO check with Willow before he committed, but Lacy's enthusiasm made no room for telephone calls. His first look at the puppies melted his heart anyway. He couldn't imagine saying no. They were mutts all right, but with adorable faces and brown eyes that pleaded for love.

"You won't be sorry. This little darlin' is going to bring so much happiness into your home," Lacy promised him, as she handed him the puppy along with a tattered, grayish towel that smelled of urine, and a small plastic bag with about one scoop of kibble.

Soon Lacy was back in her vintage Ford pick-up, spewing a cloud of blue smoke before chugging off toward the highway.

Justin glanced down at the puppy's face. What in the world had he done? Not only had he neglected to consult his wife, but they were completely unprepared to care for this pup. No food, no leash, no kennel, no toys. Nothing.

He'd have to buy all that before he brought the puppy home. Since the hardware store had shut down, however, there was no place in town to get pet supplies. Dr. Morgan might have some appropriate puppy food at his vet clinic, even though he specialized in large animals. But he wouldn't have any of the other stuff.

A drive to Hamilton was definitely in order. Which meant he had to cancel his other morning appointments and lock up his office.

He lined a cardboard banker's box with paper towels

from the restroom. After a moment's hesitation, he added the stinky towel, figuring the familiar odors would probably be comforting for the dog. Before getting in his vehicle, he gave the pup a drink of water, then set her on a patch of snow to pee. She immediately began lifting her paws, signaling she was cold.

So he set her back in her box, then proceeded to the pet store in Hamilton where he dropped almost three hundred dollars in supplies. By the time he'd made it home, it was well past noon. He carried the puppy in her new, blanket-lined crate inside the back entry.

"Hello! Anyone home?"

Not in the kitchen or adjoining dining room, though crumbs on the countertop and a jar of peanut butter suggested Willow had made a hasty lunch.

Then he heard muffled voices in the hall. A moment later, Willow appeared dressed in her winter coat and boots. She'd put on makeup and her black hair was sleek and shining. She was always pretty but he'd forgotten how absolutely stunning she looked when she got all done up.

"You look fabulous."

"Geneva and I were just going out." Her gaze dropped to the crate. "What's this?"

"I had a meeting with Lacy Stillman first thing this morning."

"From the Lazy S? She must be ancient by now."

They'd toured the ranch when they were in grade school

and Lacy had seemed so old to them then. "She's still a whirl of energy. She was headed to the animal shelter after our meeting with a litter of unwanted puppies. Somehow she talked me into taking one."

Willow's eyes widened.

"I know I should have called and checked with you. But Lacy can be pretty persuasive. And I thought having a puppy would be good for Geneva."

"You don't think we have enough to deal with?"

He wasn't sure what she meant by that, or who was included in her use of "we." Before he could ask, Geneva trailed into the room. Standing in her mother's shadow, she glanced cautiously from him to the crate he'd set on the floor.

"Want to see what's inside?" Showing Geneva the puppy before Willow agreed they should keep her wasn't playing fair. But he couldn't resist. As soon as he unlatched the crate the curious pup stuck her nose out and sniffed. Apparently deciding all was well, she stepped onto the wood plank flooring. Then, as if posing for a calendar shot, she cocked her head to one side.

"Ohhh, she's so cute," Geneva said, and even Willow smiled.

The puppy started exploring then, sniffing the floor, gobbling up the crumbs around Geneva's chair.

"What's her name?" Tentatively Geneva moved closer. "Can I pet her?"

"She doesn't have a name yet. We'll have to think of one. And sure you can pet her. If she stands still long enough."

Geneva followed the puppy as she sniffed around the kitchen perimeter. Once the pup checked out the room, she pivoted to Geneva, sniffing her hands, then allowing the girl to run her little fingers tentatively down her back.

"She's so soft. Since she likes exploring can we call her Dora?"

Justin couldn't stop smiling. It wasn't often he heard Geneva say much more than one or two words and even those only came when he asked her questions. "Fine with me. How about you, Willow?"

"I guess it's just assumed I'll agree to keep her?"

Geneva's face crumpled with dejection, but she didn't plead with her mother. Instead, she turned to him, and he realized she was looking to him to support the cause.

"Admittedly puppies are a lot of work. And I won't be here to help during the day. But the rest of the time, I'll take care of everything: the feeding, the training, getting up with her if she cries at night. If you want I could take her to the office now and then to give you a break."

Geneva's gaze swung back to her mom. Her hands were cupped under her chin in unconscious supplication.

The puppy had worked her way around to Willow now, and was sniffing her stylish black boots. Willow crouched so she could pet the little thing. "No fair ambushing me like this, Justin. How could I possibly say no?"

When she glanced up at him, though, she was smiling.

"Yay!" Geneva's squeal startled the puppy, but Dora recovered quickly, barking in reply and then running circles around the room. Geneva followed behind, laughing and trying to catch up.

Relieved, Justin decided it was safe to bring in the rest of the supplies: a container of puppy food, the plush dog bed, and a bag filled with toys and treats, as well as a harness and a leash. By the time he'd finished, Geneva's coat and boots were abandoned on the floor and she had the puppy curled up on her lap.

"Where's your mom?"

"She went to the bathroom."

He walked down the hall, past the front door and toward the bedrooms. From behind the closed bathroom door he heard the faint murmur of Willow's voice. From the way she paused occasionally, he guessed she was on the phone. She could have decided to make her call from the bathroom in case the puppy made too much noise. Or maybe she hadn't wanted to be overheard.

He put a hand on the doorknob, fighting the urge to push it open.

But besides being rude, that would solve nothing, other than annoying Willow and causing her to disconnect her call.

He went back to the kitchen and set up Dora's new food and water bowls in an unobtrusive corner. Geneva and Dora were now playing tug-of-war with one of the new rope toys. Geneva started giggling. "She's really strong, Justin!"

His new daughter's laughter was a marvelous thing, and he was enjoying it when the puppy suddenly dashed for her water bowl and began lapping madly.

"Oh, she's so thirsty!" Geneva clapped her hands together. It seemed everything the puppy did absolutely delighted her.

"We should take her outside for a pee when she's finished drinking." Justin rummaged through the shopping bag, looking for the little booties he'd purchased to protect the puppy's paws from the snow, but he was too slow. The pup had dashed from her water bowl to Geneva's coat and promptly squirted out a stream of pee.

"No, Dora!" Geneva wailed.

Before Justin had time to react, the puppy then grabbed one of Geneva's boots and began softly growling and tussling with it.

"Stop it, Dora! Stop right now or you'll make me sorry you were ever born!"

Justin had just scooped up the dog, but he froze and stared at his daughter. Suddenly he noticed Willow, standing at the point where the hall joined the kitchen. Her face was white, and her nostrils flared as she shook her head slowly at her daughter.

Gently Justin eased the boot out from Dora's teeth and handed it to Willow. Dora wiggled, wanting freedom, but he didn't set her down.

Willow went to her daughter, took her hand, and crouched so their eyes were level.

"Honey, I know you're upset with the puppy. But you shouldn't speak to her that way."

"She peed on my coat! And bited my favorite boot!"

"Dora is still a baby. We need to teach her how to behave. It's going to take a lot of patience and she might end up wrecking some stuff as she learns. Would you rather we took Dora to the animal shelter?"

Justin moved closer, bending so he was on the same level. Geneva was still pouting when she looked at Dora, then slowly she eased her hand closer and stroked the puppy's head. "I'm mad at her. But I want her to stay."

"I'm going to set up some barricades to keep the dog in this section of the house," Justin said.

"Good idea," Willow agreed.

Soon Geneva was playing with Dora again. When Willow went to put her daughter's coat in the washing machine, Justin followed.

"That was quite the scene."

Willow added a scoop of detergent to the machine, without comment.

"Where did she learn to talk that way?"

Again Willow didn't answer, but she didn't need to. It must have been Paul. Thank God Willow had finally left him. If he'd spoken to Geneva that way, Justin only wondered why she hadn't done it sooner.

"The puppy was a good idea, Justin. I just wish you'd asked me first."

"I'm sorry, but it all happened so fast. And you have to admit, she's pretty adorable."

"You've got such a kind heart." Willow touched the side of his face. "I'm afraid it's always been your weak spot."

Chapter Twenty-One

HEART POUNDING, TIFF awoke on Wednesday from a disturbing dream about Kenny Bombard. She stared at the pink walls of her bedroom seeing instead Kenny's face, dark and handsome, up close to her own. In the dream he'd been clutching her tightly and she'd felt scared, threatened, but also strangely excited.

She sat up and stared out the window, hoping a jolt of reality would clear her head. But the view didn't help. Heavy steel-gray clouds pressed down on the countryside this morning, and the snow—which had been so sparkling and fresh two days ago—now looked old and dull.

Western Montana hadn't yet experienced one of the wicked blizzards that usually struck before the holiday season, but it looked as if one might be brewing. Yet her weather app on her phone forecast only cool temperatures, low cloud cover, and moderate winds.

In the kitchen her mother was rolling out pie dough with maniacal speed. "Thanksgiving is only a few weeks away."

"Almost three weeks," Tiff pointed out as she helped herself to coffee. "Want a refill, Mom?"

Her mother shook her head. "Pies take a lot of work. I'm making apple today, tomorrow will be huckleberry. Pumpkin has to wait for the day before the holiday. You can't freeze pumpkin pie."

"Sounds like a lot of pie. How many are you expecting?" For as long as she could remember her family had invited the farm manager, and all the staff, as well as their families for Thanksgiving dinner.

Her mom consulted an open notebook on the island countertop. "Kenny of course. Bob and his wife Janet and their two sons." She glanced up at Tiff. "The boys are at that difficult age, so they could always refuse to go at the last moment. But I've got to prepare as if they'll be here."

Tiff's first sip of coffee went down like a tonic, clearing the last of the morning fog from her brain. Absentmindedly she listened as her mom continued with her list.

"…Jacob is married, but Rusty and Robin are not. So in total, counting the three of us, that makes ten adults and two teenagers."

"I guess three pies isn't so outrageous then."

"Three? I'm making six. Two of each type." Rosemary set down the rolling pin and lifted the delicate circle of pastry from the counter, expertly dropping it over a ceramic pie plate.

She made it look so easy, but Tiff knew better. "Want some help? I could peel apples."

"That's fine, dear, I know you have real work to do."

"Baking pies is real work too, but you're right—I'm a lot better at accounting." Tiff topped up her coffee and grabbed a cinnamon bun from the counter. "Where's Aunt Marsha?"

"She had appointments in Hamilton. Said she might not be home until after dinner."

"Must be a lot of errands."

"Oh, she'll probably drop in on some friends, as well. A couple of the women she went to nursing school with live in Hamilton. She visits them regularly."

It was painful to contrast her mother's life with Aunt Marsha's. Besides her work at the medi-clinic, Aunt Marsha practiced yoga, belonged to a book club, and had a full circle of friends…

"You went to college too. Do you keep up with any of your friends from those years?"

"Just Sybil. But then we've been friends forever."

"You and Sybil should go on a trip sometime." Tiff tried to think of something that would tempt her mother. "What about a gardening tour of England?"

"Maybe." There wasn't even a spark of interest in her mother's eyes as she smiled vaguely.

Tiff tried not to feel frustrated. "Well, think about it. I'm off to the barn now. I'll try to make it back for lunch."

As she left the house, her thoughts quickly shifted from her mother's mental well-being to curiosity about what she would find in the office after Kenny's late night visit.

Spade caught up to her just as she opened the barn door.

She waited for him to enter first.

"After you, sir."

She could have sworn he gave her a polite nod before slipping inside and taking the familiar route to the office door, where he sat and looked at her expectantly.

"Hang on. I'm coming." Once again she'd arrived after the workers had already gone out to the fields. Traditionally all the hardest work of the year would be finished by Thanksgiving, which made the annual feast even more of a celebration.

Once Tiff let Spade into the office, he went immediately to the rug and settled with contentment. Tiff stood in the center of the room, swiveling as she surveyed every corner. Nothing was out of place or missing that she could see. One by one she opened the filing cabinets. All looked to be perfectly in order. If any were missing, she wasn't familiar enough with them to tell.

What had he been up to last night? The puzzle nagged at her, but since there was nothing more she could do to find out, she might as well try to be productive. At least she didn't have to worry that he'd snooped on her computer, since it was password protected.

As she worked she sipped at her coffee and nibbled her way through her mother's raisin studded cinnamon bun. After a while the numbers began to blur and she sought the escape of Facebook.

Seeing nothing much of interest in her news feed she

went to her messages.

Nothing here either.

She was about to move on, when she decided to reread her old messages from Derick. When she was finished, her sense of unease for her friend deepened. There was such a difference between the friendliness of these messages and the cool reception he'd given her the other night.

Why was he shutting out, not only her, but according to Zak, his other friends, too? She understood he didn't have much free time with a new baby in his life. But she'd been right there, at his door, and he still hadn't invited her inside.

Maybe it was time she took away his options.

She closed out of her Facebook account, and logged off the computer. "Keep sleeping, Spade. I won't be gone long."

THE SPARKS CONSTRUCTION office was halfway between Lost Trail and the intersection with Highway 93, at the turnoff to the Lost Trail ski hill. The small family resort wouldn't open until they'd had enough snow, which typically happened by early December. Then this narrow mountain road would be busy, especially on weekends, as skiers took advantage of the hill's famously sweet powder and dazzling sunshine.

Some of these visitors would make their way to the Dew Drop Inn, Lolo's Pizza, and the Snowdrift Café to fuel up before and after their day on the hill. A limited selection of food and beer was available on the hill but the burgers and fries weren't nearly as tasty as those in town.

It had been years since Tiff had been skiing. When she was younger, every weekend of snow season her parents would take her and Casey out to the hill on Saturdays. Her mom would pack sandwiches and hot cocoa in a Thermos, with fruit and cookies for dessert.

Both her parents had been very good technical skiers, so she and Casey had never needed lessons, they'd learned organically by watching their mom and dad, and benefiting from the occasional tip or correction.

Because of his heart condition, Casey had to restrict himself to the easier hills. But even before she started grade school, Tiff was flying down the intermediate runs with her dad, and eventually the black diamond runs as well.

Those ski days were another family tradition that had ended with her dad's and brother's deaths.

Maybe if she'd pushed her mom to get back out there, things would have gone better for them. The fresh air and exercise might have helped bring her back from the darkness. Her mom had always laughed going down her favorite: the roly-poly run.

It would be nice to hear that laugh again.

Tiff was blinking back tears when she parked in the Sparks Construction parking lot. She should know better than to let her thoughts meander to the past like that.

Smarter to focus on the present, and what she would say to Derick when she finally saw him.

As she got out of her vehicle, she wondered how Derick felt about working at the family business. The office was beautiful, a two-story log building that served as a gorgeous prototype for the vacation homes the company was renowned for designing and constructing. A hand-carved eagle with his wings spread wide—the company logo—was astride a large wooden sign engraved with "Sparks Construction."

A half dozen vehicles were parked in the side lot, three of them white trucks with the company name and logo painted in dark hunter green. Tiff took the concrete path—brushed completely free of snow—to the entry.

She'd driven by this building countless times in her life, but had never been inside.

It made an excellent first impression.

The fieldstone fireplace at the center of the room extended a full two stories to the vaulted ceiling. A balcony with a log railing ran the perimeter of the second story, providing access to a row of individual offices. On the main floor, a woman with salt-and-pepper hair in a stylish bob sat behind a reception desk to the right of the fireplace. Behind her were massive windows looking out to the Bitterroot Mountains.

After tearing her gaze from the view, Tiff realized she knew the receptionist. Nora Morgan was married to the local vet.

"Hello, Tiff. I heard you were back. Are you planning to

build a new house?"

"Hey, Nora, yes I've been home a few days now. No plans to build a house, yet, but I would like to say hi to Derick if he's around."

"He's awfully busy these days." Nora was suddenly shifting papers on her desk. "Why don't you phone and set up a meeting?"

"Oh, I'll just be a few secs." She'd sized up the main floor and noticed two large offices to the far left of the fireplace. She could see bronze plaques on the doors and, though she couldn't read the names from here, she was willing to bet one of them was Derick's.

Tiff moved swiftly, ignoring Nora's polite request that she please wait a moment. When she was within reading range, she veered toward the door with Derick's name.

Ignoring her own qualms about her boldness, she tapped on the door and then opened it.

Derick was standing at the window, looking out at the dreary weather. As he swiveled to face her, she saw tears gleaming in his eyes. He immediately turned away, pulled out a tissue, and blew his nose.

"Damn, Tiff, you surprised me. Don't get too close, I have a cold."

Like hell.

She rested her hands on her hips and studied him. He looked utterly exhausted and stressed, totally unlike the carefree guy she'd known in school.

"Derick, what's wrong? Why are you cutting yourself off from all your friends?"

He moved around her, closing the door. "I'm not. I've just been busy."

"You didn't look that busy when I walked in."

He ran his hands through his hair and bit out in frustration, "Okay. I'm sorry I haven't replied to your messages. Will you accept my apology?"

"I didn't come here for an apology. I'm here because I'm worried about you. The last time we communicated, you sounded anxious to see me. You said—"

"Can we please not talk about those messages I sent on Facebook? Do me a favor and delete them. If Aubrey knew I'd shared all that with you she'd kill me."

"Why? You didn't say anything bad about your wife. You just shared how desperate you were to have children. That's nothing to be ashamed of."

"What a fool I was. I thought a baby would solve what was wrong between me and Aubrey. I thought it would make my parents happy and get them off our backs. Instead, the baby has made everything so much worse!"

Derick was not a guy prone to exaggeration. Yet it was hard to see how one baby could really be responsible for so many problems.

"I've heard it takes a while to adjust to a new ba—"

Derick swore. And that took her aback, too, because Derick had never been one of those guys who threw around

F-bombs to demonstrate his toughness.

"Don't talk to me about adjustment periods. Things are not going to get better."

Derick pushed up to his feet and strode back to the window. She wanted to offer him a hug, but his stiff posture was too hostile.

"I'm sorry. I'd like to help, if I could. And so would Zak. You have good friends in this town, Derick. I hope you remember that."

He kept his gaze trained out the window, jaw tense. "I have a wife to worry about now and a child. This isn't about me anymore. I should never have talked to you on Facebook. If you want to help me, keep quiet about all of it. And leave me alone."

Chapter Twenty-Two

B Y WEDNESDAY LIFE was pretty much back to normal at the sheriff's office. The press had backed off, since there'd been no new developments in the homicide investigation to feed the story. For the first time since Riley's murder, the sheriff checked in at his usual time—about an hour after the start of official office hours, no explanation offered for why he was late. Butterfield, who had a talent for taking his desk about five minutes before his boss, was the first to wish him good morning.

"Hey, Sheriff." Butterfield smoothed his tie over his rotund belly. "Was thinking I'd patrol through the Forest Reserve west of the ski hill today. We haven't done any patrols out there since hunting season started."

"Sounds good."

Zak knew Butterfield's idea of patrolling the forestry reserve involved heading to Trappers, a bar and supply shop catering to hunters and fishermen in the expansive forestry reserve to the west of the ski hill. He'd stop a few vehicles on the way, check for hunting licenses, maybe slap out a few fines, then spend the rest of the day drinking coffee and shooting the breeze with the attractive Shoshone woman who owned the establishment.

The sheriff stopped in front of Nadine's desk. She'd arrived at work the same time as Zak, and had been quietly making calls all morning trying to dig up details about Riley's life during the years between living with her friend's family and her move to Lost Trail.

"So? Any luck finding that Connor scumbag?"

Nadine squared her shoulders. Since her dressing down the other day she'd been coldly professional whenever she spoke. Zak doubted the sheriff would either notice her effort or appreciate the fact that he'd been too hard on her.

"I found the bartender who worked at Jack's Cellar when Riley was there," Nadine reported. "Claimed she was a quiet kid who worked hard, but didn't get good tips because she wouldn't flirt with the customers. She only lasted six months. He has no idea where she worked after that."

"My guess is that no-account Connor had his hooks in her by then," Butterfield offered.

"I'm still trying to find someone who knows Connor. The bartender claims he doesn't remember anyone with that name."

"You've checked into the homeless shelters and food kitchens in the area?" the sheriff asked.

"The ones closest to the bar have no record of Riley Concurran. Of course, she may not have been using her real name."

"Maybe Detective Bowering and his team will have more luck flashing her photograph around the area. Keep on it from this end, though. We need to show we put in the proper amount of effort."

Nadine flashed a look at Zak, clearly surprised the sheriff made no mention of needing to find the killer, or get justice for Riley. Just make sure no one can say the sheriff didn't do his job. Zak raised his eyebrows at her. *See what we're dealing with here?*

"I'll keep on it," Nadine said.

Zak didn't envy her assignment. Riley had lived off the grid during those years. No fixed address, no assurances she hadn't left San Francisco for that matter. All the identity she'd clung to had been her driver's license address, but she could have assumed another name in all her other dealings.

At noon the sheriff emerged from his office, placing his hat squarely on his head.

"I'm meeting the Stillman brothers for lunch. Don't call unless it's an emergency."

"An email just came in with the details from Riley's bank account," Zak said.

"I'll look at it later. Or let Black take a gander if she has time." A moment later, the sheriff was gone, the door closed, the office silent.

About a minute after they were alone, Nadine let out a long sigh. "So who are these Stillman brothers? I take it they're important?"

"Eugene and Clayton are two of the sheriff's staunchest supporters. When their mother—Lacy Stillman—passes on, they'll jointly own the biggest, most successful ranch in the area."

"Ah, that says a lot about the sheriff's priorities. Damn it, Zak. Why didn't you tell me what an idiot he was?"

"I tried to."

"Don't be so polite next time? Just flat-out say it. The sheriff is a lazy SOB who cares more about politics and his public image than solving crimes."

Zak laughed. She did have a way with words. "So you're not pissed off with me anymore?"

"I can't afford to be. You're the only other sane person working here."

"In that case, want to check out this email? It's encrypted. I'm opening it right now."

"You bet I do." Nadine stood behind him, crouching so she could peer at the screen. "Frankly I'm impressed the sheriff had enough foresight to make the request for this."

He hadn't. Zak had merely noticed Riley's debit card from Bank of America, drawn up the paperwork for a warrant, given it to the sheriff and said, "I suppose you'll be wanting to subpoena her financial records from the bank?"

The sheriff had grunted and signed, and Zak had taken over from there.

"To be honest, I wasn't expecting to get anything for at least another week. But it looks like her affairs were so simple, it didn't take long." Zak scanned the statements, then hit "Print."

Two pages spewed out from the printer on the credenza by the coffee maker. Nadine collected them, and then perched on the corner of Zak's desk.

Zak averted his gaze from her firm thigh, just inches from his hand.

"Jeez, Zak, this account wasn't even opened until early July of this year. And look at the money!"

She was close enough for him to catch a whiff of a soft, herbal scent. Was it her shampoo? As usual she wore her blonde hair securely in a bun.

He cleared his throat. *Focus.* "So about four months ago?"

"That's right. Riley opened her savings account with a deposit of five thousand dollars. After that, every week another deposit of five thousand… Where the hell would she get that kind of money?"

It seemed doubtful she'd earned that much on the street, and Zak was pretty sure she hadn't been quietly saving up under her mattress. "A drug deal?"

"It's possible, right?" Nadine glanced back at the pages. "The deposits continued until the first of September, and then they stopped."

"The bartender at Jack's Cellar described her as a quiet girl, too shy to flirt. You think a few years later she was doing major drug deals?"

"More likely she was around people doing deals and saw an opportunity to get her hands on some cash."

"You mean she stole from a dealer? That could explain why she left the city so quickly. But she didn't move to Lost Trail until the beginning of October. So where was she in September?"

"There's an ATM withdrawal in Missoula on September twenty-eighth. But nothing before that."

Zak was reading the same information on his computer screen. "Right. Next transaction isn't until October seventh when she withdrew another hundred in Lost Trail. And two weeks after that she deposits her first paycheck from Raven Farm."

"She had a lot of dough, but was living in her car. What's up with that?"

"Remember that notebook with those drawings of a house? Maybe she was saving up to buy one."

"At the rate her bank account was accumulating she already had enough for a down payment."

"I'm going to pinpoint the bank address for her branch." Zak opened Google maps on his computer. "That will give us an idea where she was living this summer at least."

"Good thinking." Nadine moved behind him, so she could see the screen. He could hear her breathing, feel her warmth, as he zoomed in on the location.

"It's in South Beach, near the AT&T baseball stadium," Zak said.

"That's in the heart of the tourist area. How close is that to Jack's Cellar?"

He dropped a pin for the bank and compared it to the pub. They were more than ten miles apart.

Nadine groaned. "Looks like Riley was hanging out in an entirely different neighborhood than we thought. I'll let Detective Bowering know about this."

"Unless, of course, she deliberately picked a bank well out of her normal stomping grounds."

Nadine rolled her eyes. "You're right. We need to consider that possibility too."

Zak watched as she headed back to her desk to call San Francisco. She may have quit the rodeo, but she still moved like an athlete, surefooted and lithe. He felt slightly buzzed, as if he'd just had a quick beer.

Nadine was smart and she was driven. It was a novel diversion to work with someone of her caliber.

But that didn't explain all his feelings for his new colleague.

Not good. He had to be careful.

✕

TIFF RACED OUT of the Sparks Construction offices, not wanting Nora, frowning behind her receptionist desk, to see the tears filling her eyes. She couldn't believe Derick would speak to anyone like that—let alone her. Once in her car, she clutched the steering wheel and waited for her whirling thoughts and emotions to calm.

She took deep breaths, turning her gaze from the building to the mountains beyond. Eventually her heart rate slowed, and her mind stopped replaying the awful things Derick had said. His goal hadn't been to hurt her. He was acting like a man backed into a terrible corner...but what was the root of the problem?

Maybe part of it was the new baby, but there had to be something more. She could think of lots of possibilities. Financial pressures with the business, disagreements between himself and his father, or deep-rooted issues in his marriage. Perhaps even all three?

She flashed back to the bruise on Aubrey's cheek. Before today she never would have believed Derick capable of hurting his wife. After what she'd just witnessed, she could no longer be so sure.

Finally she started the car and headed for home. As she drove along Tumbleweed Road toward the highway, she fought the urge to turn around for the sheriff's office. She'd love to talk to Zak and get his take on the situation.

But Derick had begged her to keep quiet and she'd already shared so much—probably too much—with Zak.

Before she knew it she'd reached the turnoff for Raven Farm. The drive had passed in a blur, proving she wasn't as calm as she'd hoped. Maybe she should work on the accounts for a bit before she went in for lunch with her mom.

What Tiff loved about accounting, what had drawn her to the career in the first place, was the way the application of logic always led to the correct answer. Emotions were not part of the equation. On a good day work brought her to a place of serenity that her personal life rarely provided.

That sensation of calm was what she was after as she settled at the scarred fir desk. She flattened her hands on the old wood and imagined her father sitting here and before him, her grandfather. So much family history was tied up on this land and in this farm.

Maybe the screw-ups that had led her to come home hadn't been such tragedies after all.

She lifted her gaze to the window, to a view that—even when gray and dull—was beautiful to her. After a few deep breaths she was ready. She opened her laptop prepared to pick up where she'd left off.

That morning she'd finished inputting all the opening balances for the Raven Farm assets, liabilities, revenues, and expenses. Now she ran a trial balance and studied the results. The farm's profits were not looking as healthy as she'd expected.

Maybe she'd made a mistake inputting data?

One way she could check the reliability of her numbers would be to reconcile the balance in the cash ledger with the most recent bank statement.

She went to the bank's website only to discover the farm didn't have online banking set up. How archaic. Fortunately she had all the information she needed to rectify the situation. As she pulled up the balances on the farm's checking and short-term investment accounts her jaw dropped.

According to her trial balance there should be over ten thousand in checking and two hundred and fifty thousand in savings. The actual amount in the checking account was within a thousand—that difference could probably be accounted for by checks that had been written by Kenny but not yet cashed by the recipient.

The difference in the savings account—a staggering eighty thousand dollars—was a different matter.

There was no reasonable explanation for the discrepancy. Where the hell was all that money?

Tiff went over the handwritten ledgers several times, to be sure she hadn't made a transposing error. Once she was certain the mistake wasn't on her end, she called the bank, only to discover banking hours had ended fifteen minutes ago.

Shoot. She hadn't realized it was that late. She'd totally blown off lunch with her mom.

Tiff went over the numbers again, then got up from the desk and walked to the window. Resting her forehead against the cool glass, she tried to think calmly and rationally.

Since the farm didn't have online banking set up before today, the bank must have been mailing Raven Farm monthly statements. A thorough search of all the filing cabinet drawers didn't reveal them though.

So where were they? Was that what Kenny had been up to the other night? Finding and concealing those statements?

If so, he obviously knew the account was out of whack. Which explained why he'd been resistant to the idea of her taking over the accounting. He was afraid of her discovering he'd been skimming cash—and a lot of it. She recalled him saying something about needing money for an operation to fix his knee. Was this how he planned to finance it?

Tiff thought about the pink underwear, and an idea occurred to her. Could Riley have found out Kenny was stealing from the farm? Maybe it was Kenny she'd met the night of her death. She might have threatened him, and he could have reacted in anger…

That would explain the sound of the vehicle her mother had heard on Halloween night.

Tiff turned from the window, suddenly anxious to clear off her desk and get back to the house before dark. She needed to talk to Zak and tell him her theory. He'd know what to do.

Chapter Twenty-Three

J USTIN MADE A pit stop at the Snowdrift Café on Thursday morning. He'd had a bad night and needed a cappuccino and fresh muffin to right himself. The puppy had been part of the problem—crying every few hours, needing to go to the bathroom, or just to be cuddled.

But his worries about Willow had been worse. He'd been foolish to think offering her his home, and his steady support for her and her daughter, would be enough for her. She was growing increasingly restless, and while he didn't believe married couples needed to be in each other's back pockets, he did feel she was keeping too many secrets.

He tried to be patient as a young mom with a baby in a stroller tried to decide what she wanted. Finally she got her mochaccino and bagel and joined the other young mothers and babies hanging out by the gas fireplace.

"Be right with you, Justin," said Patsy. "I have to pull some fresh muffins from the oven." A few moments later she set a tray on the back counter, and then turned to him.

"You look tired," she said frankly.

He pinched the bridge of his nose, rubbing out the sleep

from his eyes. "Rough night. We got a new puppy yesterday."

"Ah. One of Lacy's mutts?" Patsy didn't bother asking what he wanted. She knew. She turned on the coffee grinder, and grabbed an extra-large cup.

"Yeah. I thought a dog would be good for Geneva."

"Lucky girl. Darby and Trevor were relentless last night trying to convince us we should get one of those puppies too."

Patsy and her husband Chris had two kids, fourteen-year-old Trevor and a much younger daughter, Darby, who was six.

"You didn't give in?"

"Probably would have. But Chris is allergic. That didn't seem to matter to the kids though, selfish brats." Patsy smiled, showing no hard feelings. "Want a muffin with your latte today?"

"Make it two. No time for breakfast this morning. And since I took yesterday off to buy puppy supplies in Hamilton, I'll probably work through lunch."

"You've got it." She popped two muffins into a brown paper sack, then added a dollop of foamed milk to his triple espresso shot.

He paid, leaving a generous tip, and was about to exit when he noticed Willow and Geneva walking on the opposite side of the street.

Feeling uneasy, he paused at the window to watch. His

wife and daughter had been sitting at the breakfast table when he'd left for work, in their pajamas, but now they were both dressed. In her black leggings, smart boots, and tailored jacket, Willow looked like she belonged in a big city, not this one-horse town.

She had their daughter by the hand but Geneva was lagging. Willow paused, said something to the little girl, then took off at a march. Geneva had to skip to keep up.

Justin couldn't say why he didn't open the door and call out to them. Instead, he moved closer to the window to follow their progress. At first he thought they were headed for the library, but then he realized it was the day care.

Feeling sheepish for spying on his wife and daughter, Justin finally made his way to the street. A cold wind whipped against his face, bringing instant tears to his eyes. He had talked to Willow about using the day care if she ever wanted free time to go shopping, or to work on her photography. But with the new puppy at home, surely she wasn't planning to be out for long. He wished she'd mentioned her plans to him before he left for work.

That being said, with the puppy needing to be fed and taken out for pee, their morning had been a lot more chaotic than usual.

He could slip into the day care now, but it would probably be smarter to wait to see what Willow had to say at dinner. He didn't want her to feel he was keeping tabs on her. Even if he sort of was.

Five minutes later Justin was at his desk drafting the cod-
icil to Lacy Stillman's will. He didn't think about the puppy,
Geneva, or Willow again, until many hours later.

✕

ON HIS THURSDAY morning run, Zak's thoughts whirled
between stressing over the Riley Concurran case, and ob-
sessing about the new deputy. Usually running cleared his
head. Not today.

He couldn't help worrying that the sheriff was already
washing his hands of the case. If law enforcement in San
Francisco didn't turn up any leads—and Zak had a feeling
they wouldn't—Riley's death would soon be forgotten.

Why he cared so much, Zak couldn't say. He was just
the dispatcher, after all. And yet, he did care. Maybe he was
more passionate—and ambitious—about his career than he'd
thought.

Mind racing a lot faster than his body, Zak struggled his
way along the familiar route with his lungs burning and his
legs about as cooperative as two lumps of concrete. Checking
his stats on his watch during his cooldown he wasn't surprised to see his pace was off by more than ten minutes.

This put him in a terrible mood and matters weren't
helped when he had to line up for fifteen minutes to buy his
morning muffin. Generally Patsy was very efficient at
moving customers through her café, but the tall, distin-

guished-looking man ahead of Zak this morning seemed to have totally flustered her. First she mixed up his request for an Americano, by adding foamed milk—which meant she had to begin all over. And then, when the man—clearly a tourist, and a wealthy one, judging by his slick leather shoes and designer jeans—asked for directions to some of the popular hiking trails, she got out a piece of paper and drew him a map.

Zak wondered if Patsy would have been nearly as helpful to a homely man in a generic plaid jacket.

Finally Zak got his muffin, which he'd wolfed down by the time he was out on the street again. He glanced up and down Tumbleweed Road, trying to imagine the town from Riley's perspective. Everyone—including the sheriff and her boss at Raven Farm—seemed to take Riley's decision to make a fresh start in Lost Trail for granted. But why had she chosen this out-of-the-way town?

And what had she done, where had she hung out, when she wasn't at work or sleeping in the back of her hatchback? She wasn't a regular at the Dew Drop, according to Patsy, she rarely lingered in the coffee shop, and Cody said she always ordered her pizzas to go. It was almost as if she hadn't wanted to be seen around town.

But if that were true, why come here in the first place?

Zak studied the storefronts on Tumbleweed one more time. When he reached the corner of Carter Street, he noticed, and almost immediately discounted, the library.

However, there'd been books in her car so she must have liked to read. And hadn't Justin Pittman said last week, when he reported his meeting with the murder victim, that he'd seen her leaving the library?

Riley had received a scholarship to college, so she was no dummy. Plus the library had other advantages beyond books. First, it was warm. It was also free. And there was Wi-Fi.

One of Riley's co-workers—he thought it was Robin—had mentioned she loved *Orange is the New Black*. Maybe it wasn't the TV show Riley had liked...but the book.

Zak glanced at his watch, wondering if he could squeeze in a quick visit with Sybil Tombe. Unfortunately, due to the time he'd lost on his run and the line-up at the café there was no way. He'd have to wait for his lunch break to follow up on his hunch.

TIFF WAITED UP late on Wednesday night, wanting to talk to her aunt about the missing money in the Raven Farm's account. But by midnight her aunt still hadn't returned from Hamilton. Tiff took her book to bed where she promptly fell asleep.

Thursday morning she roused herself at the first sound of activity in the house. She pulled on a robe and went downstairs without bothering to brush her teeth or wash first. Her aunt was eating granola, fruit, and yogurt at the island.

She looked…tired.

Tiff wasn't used to seeing her aunt in anything other than top form. Marsha had been blessed with robust health, lots of energy, and generally put a positive spin on life. But something was obviously getting her down.

"Are you okay?"

"Yes, of course. Just had a long day yesterday. A friend I went to nursing school with was recently diagnosed with breast cancer. She was very upset and I wasn't able to leave her until late."

"I know. I tried to wait up for you but couldn't make it past midnight."

"I was glad to help her as best I could. I just wish I didn't have to go to work this morning."

"Maybe more caffeine will help?"

"You've said the magic word."

Marsha held out her mug and Tiff refilled it before pouring a cup for herself. She wondered if this was a good time to mention the missing money. Her aunt was obviously exhausted, plus she had a full day of work ahead of her.

Maybe she should put out some subtle feelers now, then follow up this evening over a bottle of wine.

"I'm making good progress converting the farm accounts to the computer. At first glance, though, it looks like the farm isn't making as much money as it used to."

Marsha frowned. "Are you sure? Kenny added several new customer accounts within months of being hired. If anything, I expected our revenues to be up."

"Revenues have increased. It's the profit that's unexpectedly low. But I'll take a closer look this morning. Could be I've missed something."

The view out the window this morning was much the same as yesterday. Whenever Tiff recalled her childhood in Montana, she always pictured crisp blue skies, not these heavy, brooding clouds. She turned to her aunt, who was finishing her breakfast without much enthusiasm.

"I was wondering if we could have my name added as a signatory for the business accounts at First Interstate. What do you think?"

"Of course. You could take your mother into town to do that if you can convince her to leave the house. She and I are both signatories."

"So do you, um, check the bank statements every month? Or does she?"

Marsha looked at her blankly. "I think they go directly to Kenny."

Tiff gripped the coffee mug tightly. With no one checking the actual balance in the farm bank account, it would be so easy for the manager to skim money without getting caught, as long as he maintained enough working capital to keep the business operating as normal.

"By the way, Tiff. I keep forgetting to bring this up with you, but your mom and I were discussing Riley and what should happen if the sheriff doesn't locate her next of kin."

"Yes?"

"We believe Raven Farm should pay to have her buried in the local cemetery. It seems the correct and decent thing to do."

Tiff nodded. "Want me to tell Zak to let the sheriff know?"

"Yes, and if it comes to that we'll have a small graveside ceremony as well. It's only proper and would provide closure for all of us."

"I agree. Thanks for thinking of that, Aunt Marsha."

Her aunt left for work then, and Tiff took her second cup of coffee upstairs to drink while she dressed. Even better closure than a funeral would be finding out who had killed Riley. Like so many others her aunt and mother were buying into the theory the guilty party was someone they didn't know. Someone from Riley's past life.

None of them suspected the real killer might be right under their noses...and living here on Raven Farm.

Chapter Twenty-Four

THE MORNING DRAGGED for Zak. He had lots to do, but it was mostly mundane. Homicides were good for producing paperwork, and normally he was fine with the administrative tasks of his job. But today, for the first time, he wished he had deputy status and could strike out on some official investigating of his own.

Just he and Nadine were in the office today. Butterfield was on patrol again, and the sheriff had business that had taken him to Missoula. Nadine was doggedly following up on potential leads to the man from Riley's past. She'd been on the phone with Detective Bowering a lot, speaking in a low voice, laughing occasionally.

Sounded like the two of them were having way too much fun for people investigating a homicide. Easy for Bowering to be Mr. Nice Guy. He didn't have to work with her every day. Not that Zak cared if they were overly friendly. He went back to his filing.

Once when Nadine got up to refill her coffee cup, Zak considered running his new theory past her, but the last time he'd done that he'd gotten her in hot water with the sheriff.

Better make sure he was right before he started blabbing about his ideas.

At ten minutes to twelve he got a call from Tiff on his personal phone.

"Any chance you could meet me for lunch? I'm on my way to town and there are some new developments I need to talk to you about."

Since he generally took only thirty minutes, Zak felt torn. "Could you meet me at the library? Maybe we can grab a sandwich at the Snowdrift later?"

"Sure."

"Okay. See you shortly." As he slipped the phone into his jacket pocket, Nadine looked up from her work.

"Lunch date in the library? Doesn't sound very romantic to me."

He was done denying the nature of his relationship with Tiff. "Maybe we'll check out the poetry section. Read love sonnets to each other."

She blinked in surprise, apparently this was not the answer she'd expected to hear, but she recovered quickly. "Love sonnets huh? Wow, Zak, you have hidden depths."

"I believe the term is *Renaissance man*."

THE LOST TRAIL library was in a converted two-story home donated to the town about twenty years ago by a bachelor who had died without heirs. Zak went up the stairs to a small porch where visitors were invited to remove their boots and hang their jackets. A large basket containing an array of hand-knitted slippers was positioned near the inside entrance.

Zak shucked his boots, but forewent the slippers.

Inside what would have been the living room contained displays of local fiction and nonfiction books whose subjects or authors were based in Montana. An arched opening led to the former dining room, which now contained the librarian's desk, set amid the reference section. Sybil Tombe, who had been the librarian for as long as Zak could remember, wasn't at her desk. But Zak could hear movement in the room beyond, so he walked through.

The former kitchen was now the children's nook, containing books for readers from age zero to sixteen. Sybil was tidying up the far corner, where books and cushions were strewn on the polished wooden floor.

"Hello, Zak, good timing. Thirty minutes earlier this place was swarming with preschoolers and their stressed-out parents." Sybil was a petite woman, under five feet, with a curvy figure, curly grayish-blonde hair, and a penchant for eyeglasses that made a statement. Today she wore dark purple, circular frames that gave her an owlish appearance.

"Looks like they had a fun time." He picked up a few of the cushions and added them to the stack in the corner.

"Oh they did—once we pried their iPads away from

them." Sybil shook her head ruefully. "Today we had a toddler with a bottle in one hand and a device in the other. And the little guy was scrolling like an expert."

"Crazy."

"I'll say. Children are being exposed to the Internet and video game world much too young in my opinion. But I guess I should be thankful their parents still think it's worthwhile to expose them to books as well." She tucked the hardcover book in her hands into the stack on a wheeled cart, then pushed it against the wall.

"Now how can I help you, Zak? Do you have a book you need me to find?"

Thanks to Sybil's help, he'd worked his way through almost the entire reading list of MU's Criminology program. She kept bugging him to take actual correspondence courses and earn credits, but Zak didn't figure he'd ever need the degree. But maybe Sybil had a point. It wasn't too late, if he changed his mind.

"Not this time, Mrs. T. I'm here to ask about the woman who was murdered—Riley Concurran. But maybe someone from the sheriff's office has already talked to you about her?"

He wasn't surprised when she shook her head. He hadn't seen her name in any of the investigation reports he'd filed.

"No. No one's asked me anything. But I'm afraid I wouldn't have had much to say if they had."

Damn. So much for his hunch. "You never saw her in the library?"

"Oh, I saw her all the time. She used to spend hours here. I just meant I have no information to help find her killer. She was always alone and so quiet. I tried a few times to get her to open up to me, but to be honest, Zak, she seemed almost scared to make friends."

"What would she like do when she was here?"

"She always headed straight upstairs. Sometimes I'd find her reading in one of the easy chairs in the fiction section. Other times she was at one of the computers."

"Can you show me?"

"Of course."

He followed her back to the foyer, but just as they were about to go up the narrow oak staircase, the bell at the front door rang and in came Tiff, wearing a warm parka and black leather boots.

"Hey there, Mrs. T., Zak." She unwound a red scarf from her neck. "I hear a big storm front is moving in from the coast. Supposed to bring about a foot of powder to-night."

"Oh boy, I figured we were about due for a good old-fashioned blizzard. How are you, dear?" Sybil gave Tiff a hug. "It was so nice to see you at church with your mother on Sunday. I could tell Rosemary was happy to have you by her side."

"Thanks, Mrs. T. It's amazing to me that you and Aunt Marsha never seem to age. What's the secret?"

Zak noticed she didn't put her mother in the same category.

"Clean living and hard work?" Mrs. T. quipped. Then she laughed. "Oh, we're aging all right, Tiff, and one day it's going to catch up with us." Her expression grew serious. "How have you found your mom since you got home?"

"Not very well, to be honest."

"I'm so sorry. They say time heals all wounds, but it's not always so." Sybil patted her shoulder, then added, "I was just going upstairs to help Zak with something. I'll be right back."

"Actually, Tiff might be interested, too," Zak said. "Riley worked on Raven Farm so Tiff has an interest. And none of this is official business. I'm just asking as a private citizen, Ms. T. I'm just the dispatcher not a deputized officer of the law."

"Yes, I know, Zak. A real underutilization of your God-given intelligence and talents, if you ask me. Regardless, I'm happy to tell you what little I know."

As they followed Sybil up the stairs, Zak gave Tiff a quick run-down.

"In trying to get a bead on the kind of woman Riley was, I figured it would help to find out where she spent her time when she wasn't sleeping or working at the farm. Just today it occurred to me that the library was an obvious choice for someone who doesn't have a home or much money."

"Good thinking."

"Can't believe it took me this long."

"No one else in the sheriff's office thought to check out the library," Tiff pointed out.

At the top landing, Sybil went past the unisex restroom. The doors to the three former bedrooms had been removed to allow for better traffic flow. In the first room was the nonfiction collection. Sybil bypassed this in favor of the next room, which housed fiction. She pointed to two armchairs located under the double-sash window.

"Riley would sit here and read for hours on the weekend. She powered through *Orange is the New Black* in one day. She was no trouble, but I couldn't help wondering why she spent so much time here instead of home."

"She didn't have a home," Zak said. "Riley was sleeping in her car."

"She did seem so lost and lonely," Sybil said thoughtful-ly. "I regret so much that I wasn't able to earn her trust and get her to confide in me. Young people often think their problems are insurmountable, when in fact, solutions are available, if they would just reach out for help."

Tiff brushed her fingers over the chair's faded burgundy velvet upholstery. "It's so sad. I wonder if I'd come home earlier, if I'd met her, maybe I could have helped..."

Zak glanced around the room. There was nothing more he needed here. But if she'd spent time on the Internet, she'd probably left a trail. "Can we take a look at the computers?"

"Yes. We have three of them in the study room." Sybil led them to the final and largest room, with two windows facing the street. A long rectangular table with chairs occupied the center of the room. Against the far wall were three computer stations. Sybil indicated the one in the far back corner. "This was her favorite."

"Thanks, Mrs. T." Zak sat in the cubicle she'd pointed out. "Mind if I play around for a while?"

"Here's the access code." Mrs. T. handed him a slip of paper with random letters and numbers. "Go right ahead. I need to get back to my desk now, but let me know if you have any other questions." With a final warm smile for Tiff she let them be.

Tiff grabbed a chair from the long table and pulled it close to Zak. "What are you hoping to find?"

"Not sure. I'm going to review the browsing history. Hope something pops out."

He felt Tiff peering over his shoulder. "How helpful that the dates are listed. You can rule out all the searches after her death."

"Yup. I figure the key dates should be the last week of October."

He pulled a notebook from his jacket pocket and a pen. Some of the searches were obviously for school projects. He discounted one for themes in Shakespeare's tragedies, another on Steinbeck's *Grapes of Wrath*, and a third on interesting science projects for middle school students. Lots of searches on weather, travel, and road conditions he also disregarded.

Anything a bit unusual or interesting he copied down. Soon he had an entire page filled. Tiff read them out loud.

"Rotten Tomatoes, movies playing in Hamilton, movies playing in Missoula, cupping therapy for pain management, signs of strep throat, signs you have cancer, fetal alcohol syndrome, meth, where to get weed, where to get a hunting license, when is hunting season, how to avoid getting pregnant, what to do if you're pregnant, single mothers, rights of birth mother, celebrity news, *People* magazine, *US* magazine, country music hits, cute animal pictures, funny cat videos, finding a lawyer, recipes to lose weight, exercise to lose weight."

And there was a lot more, which Zak felt safe ignoring.

When she'd read through the list, Tiff asked, "Well? Anything jump out at you?"

"To be honest, I was hoping to find a name."

"Someone she was trying to find?"

"Exactly. Everyone in this town who knew her, even a little bit, claims she came here to make a fresh start. But why pick Lost Trail? That's what I don't get. It's such a small, out-of-the-way place. She must have had a reason. And in my mind that reason is most likely a person. Someone she knew. Or wanted to know."

"Ah…like maybe she was trying to track down her birth father? Something like that?"

Zak turned to look at Tiff, impressed. "Yes. That's brilliant. According to the friend whose family took Riley in, her father was never in the picture. That must have weighed on her."

"Especially after her mother died."

"But her mother died years ago. Why go searching for her dad now?"

"Maybe this was the first time she had the money?"

Zak thought about all those cash deposits from the summer. "You could well be right. But if she was looking for her father you'd think she'd be talking to people—not shying away from them."

He glanced at his watch. "Damn. I need to be getting back. Sorry I don't have time to grab a sandwich. What was it you wanted to talk about?"

Tiff hesitated. "There are two things actually. The first is easiest. Mom and Aunt Marsha wanted me to tell you that if no next of kin claims Riley's body, our family will pay to have a service and burial here in Lost Trail."

"That's decent of them. I'll let the sheriff know."

"Thanks…" She fussed with the ends of her scarf. "The other thing…this is just between us, Zak. I'm not sure if I'm over-reacting but there is something suspicious going on with Kenny."

"You talking about the possibility he had sex with Riley? And your hunch he might have driven away from the farm the night of the murder?"

"There's something else, as well. Just yesterday I found out someone's been skimming thousands of dollars from the farm's investment account."

Zak tensed. "Kenny?"

"I can't be certain yet, I need to go back further into the records. But yes, it's probably Kenny. Do you think it's possible he was having an affair with Riley and she somehow found out he was stealing from our business? Maybe Kenny set up a late-night rendezvous with her, trying to convince her to keep quiet, and when she wouldn't, he lost his temper and hit her?"

Zak looked at his friend with concern. "Sounds like a solid theory to me. You need to make an official report of this."

"I'm not ready to do that yet. I need to check the older records first. But as soon as I'm confident I'm right, I'll come by your office."

"Make sure that you do."

Chapter Twenty-Five

"I'VE FOUND HIS last name." Nadine put down the phone and punched a fist into the air.

Zak looked up from his computer screen. "Connor's?"

"Yes. It's O'Leary. I finally tracked down a young woman who'd worked at Jack's Cellar at the same time as Riley. This girl and her boyfriend at the time went out with Riley and Connor once…and she actually remembered Connor's last name."

"That's a lucky break. Not many would remember the first name, let alone the last name of someone you'd met just once, four years ago."

"She said the name was memorable because she and her boyfriend thought Connor was a jerk and felt his last name was appropriate because he was always leering at women who didn't belong to him."

"Good work," Zak said, but Nadine was already making a second call and held up her hand to silence him.

"Hey, Detective, this is Deputy Black from Lost Trail…" She paused as something was said on the other end. From her smile, and the way she started patted her hair with her free hand, Zak guessed the detective was letting her know he was glad to hear from her.

"Me too," she said, in response to whatever it was the detective had said. Then she got to business. "I've got a last name for Riley's boyfriend. It's O'Leary." Another pause. "Yes, Connor O'Leary."

A longer pause this time, during which time Zak supposed the detective was promising to check into the guy and get back to her.

"Thanks. I appreciate that."

Another smile. Another stroke of her hair, and then she was hanging up. Hurriedly Zak pinned his gaze back on his notes.

"So," he opened, a few minutes later when she hadn't said anything. "You going to tell the sheriff you found the ex-boyfriend?"

"Not until I hear back from California and have followed the lead as far as I can. I'm not going to get caught flat-footed again." She tapped a furious rhythm with her pen against a pad of paper, then sprang out of her chair and went for some coffee.

He could sense her pent-up adrenaline. Hanging tight and waiting was often the hardest part of this job. "Hopefully the detective gets back to you soon."

"He's in the middle of something urgent right now. He promised to get me some information by tomorrow morning, though. This could be our big break..."

Zak empathized. She was trying so hard to impress her boss by proving Ford's pet theory. But Zak was more convinced than ever that it was trouble in Lost Trail—not from her past—that had led Riley to her death. If he turned out to be wrong, then fine. Getting justice for Riley was what it was all about.

But Zak didn't think he'd be wrong.

If Riley had simply been running from trouble she would have been smarter to pick a bigger town or city, where it would be easier to blend in.

Instead, she'd chosen Lost Trail. And there had to be a reason. Possibly she was trying to find her father. But maybe it had been a romantic interest that had brought her here.

Since his lunch break he'd been checking into Kenny Bombard's past, trying to find a link between the former ski guide and Riley, a place or time when their lives might have intersected. So far he'd found nothing, but that didn't mean the connection wasn't out there, waiting to be discovered.

THE PITIFUL CRYING of a puppy was Justin's first sign something was wrong when he let himself in through the back entrance of his home. He'd left his law office an hour earlier than usual, worn out after a day of worrying about Willow. He wasn't sure why he'd been so reluctant to just call her after he spotted her dropping Geneva off at the day care. Was he trying to prove to himself that he trusted her? Or was he simply too afraid about what she'd say if cornered?

"Hey, Dora. It's okay. I'm coming to get you." He tramped fresh snowflakes onto the kitchen floor as he rushed to the crate on the other side of the room. As soon as he unlatched the door, the puppy hurled her body at him, whining and wagging her tail with furious intensity. Inside the crate she'd knocked over the bowls of water and food Willow had left for her. The newspapers piled in the far corner reeked of urine.

He cradled the puppy to his chest as he carried her outside. When she seemed a bit calmer, he set her down to do her business, but the snow—which had started falling about an hour earlier—was too much of a distraction. She batted at the flakes, then, finally appreciating her freedom, began racing in circles around the frozen yard.

Justin watched with a faint smile, tamping the growing ball of anxiety in his gut as he tried to figure out where Willow and Geneva were.

Willow's car was in the driveway in its usual spot.

But clearly she wasn't home.

To confirm this, once the puppy had calmed down enough to defecate on what in springtime would hopefully be a bed of tulips, Justin toured each room of the house. Silence and emptiness greeted him.

He ended in the master bedroom. Willow's bathrobe was on its usual hook. He opened a few drawers and found all her sweaters, T-shirts, and socks, neatly stacked. In the bathroom her pink toothbrush was next to his green one. Her shampoo and conditioner bottles were still in the shower.

He was about to check the basement when his cell phone rang. The name on the display was the Little Cow Pokes Day Care.

"Hello?"

"Justin? This is Debbie-Ann."

Debbie-Ann had opened the day care ten years ago, to support herself financially after her daughter Ashley was born.

"Your wife told me you'd be picking up Geneva at five," she continued, "but I was hoping you could come a few minutes earlier? My daughter's car-pool ride just canceled and if possible I'd like to drive her to her ballet class in Hamilton. Geneva's our last wee one, and I think she's more than ready to come home. It's been a long day for her."

Justin blinked, processing the rapid flow of information. "I'll be there in five minutes."

"Thanks so much."

Fingers flying he sent a text message to Willow asking where she was. As he dressed to go out in the storm again, he kept looking at his phone, praying she would reply. But there was nothing.

He contemplated what to do with the pup. He didn't have the heart to put her back in that crate, so he'd have to bring her with him. He wrapped a flannel blanket around Dora, then took off across the back alley, running the four blocks to the day care.

Debbie-Ann had Geneva bundled into her snowsuit and boots by the time he arrived. In her hands Geneva clutched a painting on a large piece of poster paper. The moment she spotted the puppy though, she dropped the art and went to Dora, patting her gently on the head.

"You're a doll," Debbie-Ann said. "I hope it wasn't too much of an inconvenience to leave work early?"

"Not at all. I was already home actually. Willow forgot to tell me I was supposed to pick up our daughter."

Debbie-Ann frowned and might have asked more questions if she hadn't been in such a hurry. She picked the painting up from the floor and handed it to Justin. Geneva had painted a mother and a little girl holding hands on one side of the paper. On the other side was a big blob, which she'd made with heavy slashes of black ink.

The sight of it almost made him sick. What had Debbie-Ann made of this? And what in the world had prompted Geneva to create it?

Debbie-Ann stooped in front of Geneva. "Good-bye, honey. I hope you come and see us again soon."

Geneva said nothing, just stared at her solemnly.

"Thanks for everything," Justin said. "Good luck making that ballet class." He led his daughter outside where she immediately cringed as the cold air and snow pelted her face.

"I'm sorry I didn't bring the car. Want to ride piggy-back?"

She nodded, so he crouched low enough that she could circle her arms around his neck and her legs around his waist. He felt her hide her face against the back of his parka. Still holding the dog in one arm, and Geneva's painting in the other hand, Justin loped for home.

Once back in the warmth of the house, Justin waited for Geneva to ask about her mother. But she seemed content to throw toys for the puppy, who attacked each of them in turn.

"Are you hungry?"

"No. We had apples and cheese for a snack."

"Were there any other kids at the day care with you?"

"In the morning there were five kids and two babies. After lunch the babies went home. And then the other kids did too."

"Were they nice, the other kids? Did you play with them?"

Geneva looked at him and shrugged, then tossed another of the puppy's stuffed toys, which sent Dora on the chase.

Justin sent a second message to Willow, then cleaned up the mess in the crate, and put a frozen lasagna in the oven for dinner. He kept waiting for Geneva to mention her mother, not wanting to upset her by raising the subject first. After they'd finished dinner he set up Geneva with a movie, and paced the house anxiously, every few minutes looking out at the street—surely Willow had to come home soon.

None of his text messages had been answered, so finally he tried calling her. A few seconds after hitting the green connect button, he heard a faint ringing coming from the other end of the house. He followed the sound to one of Willow's coats, hanging by the front door. Reaching into the pocket, he found her phone.

For the first time it occurred to him that something terrible might have happened to her.

He thought about the young woman who'd been murdered, a little over a week ago. Could it have happened again?

With his heart banging against his chest, he found the number to the sheriff's office, then hesitated before hitting the green connect button. There was one last place he ought to check. Racing downstairs he went to the storage room and the boxes of stuff Willow had brought with her when she moved in. He reached for the one that held what had once been her most treasured possession—her camera.

The box was still there, but the camera case had been replaced with a note.

I'm fine. Don't try to find me.

Chapter Twenty-Six

I T WAS AFTER six and dark when Zak locked up the sheriff's office. The forecast blizzard had arrived and as he made his way to his truck snow pelted from the sky, biting at every exposed inch of skin on his face and neck. He ducked his head against the onslaught as he fumbled for his keys.

Once he had his vehicle started he brushed the snow from the windows and scraped ice from the windshield. Despite his gloves, his fingers were prickling from the cold by the time he was done.

He drove home slowly, along roads with at least five inches of fresh powder. This stuff was great for the ski hill, brutal for driving. He hoped people would be cautious and there wouldn't be any accidents tonight.

As he drove, he thought about Riley, a stranger in town, who worked hard all day at the Christmas tree farm, and spent her off-hours in the library, evenings sleeping in the back of her hatchback. It sounded like such a lonely existence.

Had she had hopes and dreams for her future? The sketchbook with the drawings of a modest, but attractive home, suggested she had…

As he turned onto Winding Down Way he paused by Miss Christensen's place. A faint light shone from the living room, and a bluish glare told him the TV was on. Must be a lonely existence for her, with no husband or children, and very few contemporaries still alive to socialize with.

A flash of light from the cemetery on the other side of the road made him curious. He pulled over and killed the engine. A minute later two teenagers came running down the hill, wearing head lamps, ducking behind tombstones and tossing snowballs at one another. When they got closer to the road, they aimed a few of their missiles at the house across the way.

One hit the living room picture window, squarely in the middle.

Zak wondered if Miss Christensen would come out to the stoop, shaking her fist. But instead she drew the curtains closed.

The boys—for they were close enough to the streetlamps now that he could see their faces—retaliated with another volley.

Zak sighed, then got out of his truck. The boys immediately started running, each in opposite directions, but they froze when he called out their names. "Trevor! Darren! I'm going to be phoning your parents tomorrow unless you come talk to me now."

Darren started running again, maybe he hadn't heard

him, or perhaps he preferred to take his chances with his parents. Trevor Larkin, however, pulled off his head lamp and came trudging through the snow.

"Hey, man, we were just having fun. Snowballs don't hurt anything."

"No. And they're a lot easier to clean up than, say, a raw egg."

Trevor cringed, which told Zak his hunch had been correct.

"Please don't tell my dad. He's super stressed these days. He'll be pissed off as hell if he finds out. It was just supposed to be a prank."

Zak put a hand on the boy's shoulder. "I don't want to make trouble for you, Trevor. But I believe you may have seen something on Halloween night that you should have told the sheriff about."

Trevor's eyes widened. "How did you know?" Then, as if realizing he'd made a tactical error: "I didn't see anything. Not really."

The boy was trembling now, whether from fear or the cold, Zak couldn't tell. But he'd had enough of this frigid air himself. "My truck is warm. Let's talk in there and then I'll give you a lift home."

Trevor didn't argue. Once the boy was in the passenger seat, Zak turned on the engine and jacked up the heat.

"Miss Christensen told me those eggs were thrown after two in the morning."

"Maybe. We weren't keeping track of time. I'd turned off my phone so I wouldn't hear my mom when she texted me."

"What was the plan? Tell her your phone died and you lost track of time?"

Trevor flushed. "We were having fun. And we weren't hurting anyone."

"You were still out pretty late. Streets must have been dead at that hour."

"They were. It was so cool. We only saw one—" He stopped abruptly. "I'd never been out so late before. I liked it."

"Tell me everything you and Darren did and saw after you egged Miss Christensen's window."

Trevor squirmed. "I can't really remember."

"You know a woman was killed that night, right? This is important."

The boy let out a shaky breath. "We ran along Winding Down Way until we got to Second Street, then we went up to Tumbleweed. We were walking in the middle of the street because there was literally no one around. Just when we were about to split up to head home we saw a truck coming down from Lost Creek Road. We jumped off the road, thinking it was heading downtown, but then the truck turned into the alley and ended up behind the medical clinic."

"Did the driver see you?"

"I don't think so. We saw the lights coming from a long way off and made sure we were out of sight."

"Could you see the parking lot behind the medical clinic?"

"Part of it. It looked like the driver rolled something out of the truck. I couldn't tell what. It was dark and I was getting spooked. Darren was already gone and that's when I took off for home, too."

Zak berated himself for not following up on the vandalism sooner. He should have realized the kids might have seen something useful.

"Can you tell me anything about the truck, or the driver?"

Trevor shook his head. "No. It was too dark."

Zak couldn't decide whether to believe him. He stared at Trevor, waiting to see if he would buckle under the pressure. Change his story.

The kid remained silent.

"Okay, Trevor, I'm going to drive you home. But you better tell your folks about this. I'll expect you and at least one of your parents to come into the sheriff's office tomorrow to make a statement."

AN HOUR BEFORE Geneva's bedtime, Justin realized he couldn't wait for his daughter to bring up the subject of her missing mother. They needed to talk about it now. He sat next to her on the sofa. Exhausted after hours of playing,

Dora was snoozing on her lap. He stroked the puppy's soft coat.

"She's so cute when she's sleeping. Are you glad we kept her?"

Geneva kissed the top of the puppy's head. "I love her."

"Honey, what did your mom say to you when she dropped you off at the day care? Did she tell you where she was going?"

Geneva cast her gaze down. A few seconds later a tear dropped onto the puppy's back. In that moment Justin felt pain like he'd never known before. He took Geneva's hand and gave it a tender squeeze.

"S-she said she had to go away. That she would be gone a long time."

"I'm sorry, honey. That must have made you sad."

She nodded. "She said I couldn't come. I had to stay with you."

He heard fear in her voice, sensed it in her tense little body.

He had to say something and pray he found the right words. "For a long time I wanted to be a daddy to a little girl—a little girl just like you. I didn't think it was going to happen, but then one day you and your mom showed up at my house. And since you moved in I've been so happy."

Geneva didn't look at him, but he could tell she was listening carefully.

"I don't know what your life was like before you moved

here, but I promise I will take care of you and I'll love you. I'll never touch you unless you want a hug or a piggyback ride, or some kind of help from me. I might get upset at times but I'll never hurt you or yell at you."

Slowly Geneva lifted her head and glanced at him sideways. Her long brown lashes still gleamed with tears. But he thought he could see the beginning of trust in her eyes.

"I hope your mom comes back soon. I know you'll miss her until she does. But you are going to be safe with me. You, me, Grandpa Clark, and Dora…we're a family and we'll stick together."

Geneva's lips trembled. "B-but what about when you're working?"

"We'll have a new routine. I'll walk with you to day care every morning and pick you up again before dinner. The rest of the time—the evenings and mornings and weekends—we'll be together. Does that sound okay to you?"

She nodded, and looked like she was going to say yes, but instead she burst into tears. The puppy, disgruntled, climbed off her lap, but she didn't notice. Watching her shoulders heave with her sobs, Justin felt helpless. He'd made such a complete mess of things with this talk.

But then she flung her arms around him, and clung to him, and he realized no—this was good. Crying was much healthier than silence. This was going to be a process, but he and his daughter had survived the first step.

✕

WATSON WAS WAITING by the window when Zak got home, curled up on the window ledge, keeping an eye on the world. He did not come running to greet Zak, the way a dog would do, and Zak respected him for this.

Cats excelled at both dignity and self-preservation. When he was growing up Zak's family had both a dog and a cat. The dog had developed a mean streak, an inevitable result of being on the wrong end of Zak's father's boot too many times.

Not so the cat, who'd been smart enough to make himself scarce whenever the patriarch of the family was around. A small boy in a tough family could learn a lot from a cat. And Zak had.

But maybe he'd learned his lesson too well. He'd liked his dispatcher job because it kept him out of the fray. But it also hampered his ability to be effective. If he'd been wearing a deputy badge when he'd picked up Trevor, he would have been able to knock on his parents' door and insist on getting a statement, right then and there while Trevor was still edgy and afraid.

Zak put together a healthy stir-fry for dinner: chicken, bok choy, some mushrooms, and a dash of peanut sauce. He had to make up for the nights of indulging in burgers with Tiff. Dietary lapses aside, he was glad she'd moved back. Their friendship was like a pair of comfortable old slippers—

they still fit, even though they hadn't been worn in years.

After he'd finished eating, Zak made some notes about his encounter with the boys that night and his conversation with Trevor. He hoped the boy didn't chicken out tomorrow and go back on his promise to tell his folks what had happened—and more importantly, tell the sheriff, too.

Zak wondered if the sheriff would be able to pull more details from Trevor. He was sure the kid had seen more than he'd admitted. He sent a text message to Tiff, asking the color and make of Kenny Lombard's vehicle. Her response was terse: *Black Dodge Ram.*

Zak took a deep breath. This case would really come together if Trevor could at least confirm the color of the truck. Kenny must have known where Riley parked her car at night. He'd met her there and they'd had an argument. When he hit her, Kenny might not have realized his own strength. The fact that he hadn't left the body where it was, but had dropped it off outside the medi-clinic seemed to indicate some level of remorse.

Of course, the truck Trevor had seen might not have been Kenny's, but someone who lived on Lost Creek Road.

First on the street was Dr. Pittman, the coroner, and then Derick and Aubrey. The next house belonged to Dr. Morgan, the local vet, and his wife Nora, who worked for the Sparks family. After the Morgan's was a vacant home, currently for sale, followed by the Fitzgeralds who owned the pharmacy. Finally there was the largest home of all, the one belonging to Derick's parents, Will and Jen.

But what link did any of those people have with Riley?

A vague memory teased Zak, something that had been listed in the inventory of items in Riley's car. That report had been long filed and none of the contents deemed worthy of follow-up. He was the only one who'd considered the notebook worthy of interest. But there'd been a pen clipped to that notebook. And there had been something familiar about that pen…

An idea popped into his head. Was it possible?

Deciding he wasn't going to sleep until he tested his theory, Zak pulled on his boots and jacket, despite Watson's aggrieved look.

"Sorry, buddy. Duty calls." Wind and snow blasted his body the moment he stepped outdoors. Another two inches of snow had settled on his truck during the time it had taken him to prepare and eat his dinner. Methodically he brushed the truck clean, then carefully drove the snow-covered roads back to the office.

Once inside it took only minutes to find the photographs he was looking for. He scrolled through pictures of Riley's sleeping bag, the duffel bag with her clothing, running shoes, a couple of books. And then the notebook, with the pen still attached. A white pen with a green logo.

Zak zoomed in on the logo until he could read the printed letters: *Sparks Construction.*

Was it possible Riley had visited the office, to inquire

about building her dream home? But Sparks Construction specialized in luxury homes, nothing near as modest as the place Riley had sketched out.

As he puzzled over this, Zak reviewed the search terms he'd copied from the library computer that afternoon. He went over the list once, twice, and on the third time a phrase jumped out at him, followed immediately by a theory that was so preposterous it couldn't be true.

And yet…it would explain why Riley had come to the town of Lost Trail and not any other place. It would explain where she got that pen. And why she'd opened a new bank account with those fat cash deposits.

Zak drew a heavy black line under the words: *rights of a birth mother.*

On its own, the phrase didn't mean much. But add in some other curious coincidences, like Derick and Aubrey adopting a child practically out of the blue at the beginning of September. Derick and Aubrey acting like happy, doting parents for the first month, then becoming nervous hermits around the beginning of October—after Riley Concurran moved to town.

Riley Concurran, the birth mother of their baby. What deal had they struck with her? Had it been legal? Zak suspected not. No, he guessed they'd paid her for the baby— in weekly five thousand dollar increments that wouldn't raise the curiosity of anyone at the bank—and in return Riley had agreed to stay out of their lives.

Only she hadn't. Why? Did she come seeking more money or because she regretted giving away her child? The sketchbook of her dream home—it had included a room with a crib. Why hadn't he picked up on that earlier? If Riley had wanted her baby back, what would that have done to Derick and Aubrey—and their marriage?

According to Tiff, Derick's wife had been on the verge of leaving him because they couldn't have a child. And he'd been under pressure from his folks, too, who were desperate for a grandchild…and an heir to the family business.

Derick must have arranged to meet Riley. And when she insisted she wanted the baby back…Derick must have gone into a rage and hit her.

That part was hard for Zak to imagine. It just didn't fit the character of the guy he'd grown up with. But there'd been that bruise on Aubrey's face. So maybe Derick had changed, buckling under pressure that was too much for him to bear.

That had to be it.

And yet, it still didn't feel right. Later that night, in bed, listening to the howling storm outside his window, Zak continued to play with his theory, twisting it this way and that, trying to figure out why it didn't ring true.

And then, just as he was drifting to sleep, a new idea emerged, the way wispy water particles clotting together form a cloud on the peak of a mountain.

Chapter Twenty-Seven

A S A RULE Zak ran every morning regardless of the weather. But his anxiety about whether Trevor and his parents would show up to give a statement—as well as the fresh foot of snow on the ground, and temperatures cratered at a frigid minus twenty—convinced him it would be better to get into work early. His revised theory about Riley's murder still sounded incredibly farfetched to him. And based, as it was, on circumstantial evidence—a pen, a hunch about those bank transactions, a phrase used for an Internet search—Zak knew there was no way he was going to convince Sheriff Ford to follow up on it.

And yet, in his gut, he felt he was right.

His only hope of convincing anyone was if Trevor came in to make a statement—and if Zak could convince him to say more than he had last night.

Zak added fresh kibble and water to Watson's bowls. As he made his exit, Watson, already stationed on his window ledge, gave him his usual blank stare by means of farewell.

The bitter cold air stung his face and lungs as he dashed for his truck. A brilliant red glow on the eastern horizon foreshadowed the upcoming dawn, but the streets were still dark as Zak drove his usual route to work. At least the snow had stopped and the plow had been out sometime early that morning.

In the office Zak put on coffee, then went over the steps of logic that had led him to his eureka moment last night.

He went over all the evidence: the preliminary autopsy, the crime-scene photos, the bank records and written statements that made up the official evidentiary trail, and then his own notes.

To him, his theory held. He longed to blurt out everything to Nadine, when she came in twenty minutes after eight, swearing because she'd forgotten to plug in her SUV and had needed a boost from her neighbor to get it started.

But if Trevor didn't show up, how would he prove it?

He decided to keep quiet, though his nerves were so jittery, he couldn't sit still for more than a few minutes at a time.

"What's with you?" Nadine asked as she poured her first coffee. "You're flitting around like a riled-up hornet this morning."

He shut the filing cabinet. "Just putting away a few things."

"Huh." She gave him a suspicious look, but went back to her desk and said nothing more about it.

Half an hour later Butterfield arrived, followed, mere minutes later, by the sheriff. Everyone's first action was to grab hot coffee and complain about the weather.

"It's not even officially winter yet," Nadine grouched.

"Bet you're missing the rodeo life now," Butterfield taunted. "You could be in Vegas, gearing up for the rodeo finals."

"Those day are over and I'm okay with it." Nadine glanced at the phone, obviously anticipating a call from the detective in California.

Zak empathized with her anxiousness. No rush on earth matched this feeling of being on the verge of solving a case. He didn't care about scoring points with the sheriff, being first over the line. If he could have nudged Nadine into supporting his theory, he would have gladly done so, and let her take as much limelight as she wanted. But his theory was so far-out he knew no one was going to believe him, unless…

Come on, Trevor. Do the right thing.

Time ticked along with excruciating slowness. Finally, at quarter to nine, stuff started happening fast. Trevor and his mother came in at the exact moment as the phone on Nadine's desk started to ring.

She jumped on it. "Deputy Black here."

Meanwhile Zak sprang from his chair, beyond relieved Trevor had followed through. "Morning, Patsy, Trevor. Cold one, isn't it?"

Patsy put her hand protectively on her son's shoulder. Usually a bright, cheerful person, she was looking grim and worried. "We need to talk to the sheriff."

"Hang on a sec." Zak went to the open door. Sheriff Ford was at his desk, scowling at the paperwork Zak had left there for him to sign. "Patsy Larkin's here with her son Trevor. He needs to talk to you about something he saw on Halloween night. Around the time of the homicide."

"How the hell do you know what they want to talk about?" Butterfield barked.

The sheriff's frown lines deepened. "All right. Bring 'em in."

As Zak waved the mother and her son into the office he noticed Nadine still huddled over her phone.

Sheriff Ford put on the smile he reserved for voting citizens of Bitterroot County and got up to usher his visitors into chairs. "Hell of a morning, isn't it? How are you doing, Patsy? Trevor? Everything good at home?"

Patsy was pale and not prepared for small talk. "My son needs to tell you what he saw the night that woman was killed."

The sheriff's gaze flew up to Zak, as if to say, *What the hell is this about? Why didn't you prepare me?*

A little preamble was in order. Hanging back, near the door, Zak said, "I ran into Trevor last night and we had a chat. He'd been out late on Halloween night and saw something. It didn't seem important to him at the time, but since we now know Riley Concurran was murdered around the same time he was walking home, I suggested he come in this morning and talk to you about it."

Eyebrows still floating high on his forehead, the sheriff shifted his scrutiny back to the teenager and waited.

"Um. Like Zak said, it was late. Around three in the morning."

Patsy turned to her son. "You never told me you were out *that* late."

Trevor shrugged. "We weren't doing anything wrong." His gaze shifted to Zak briefly. "Well, not really. Maybe threw an egg or two. That's all. On the way home we—I mean, I—saw this truck turn onto Tumbleweed from Lost Creek Road. I ducked into the doorway for the dentist's office, and waited for the truck to pass, but it didn't. Instead the driver turned onto the back alley and stopped behind the clinic. I started walking again and that was when I noticed a big guy get out of the truck and roll something out of the back of the truck onto the ground."

The sheriff stared at him a long time before finally asking a question. "Who else was in the truck?"

"No one, just the driver."

"And did you recognize the driver?"

Trevor stared down at his boots. "No, sir."

"Could you tell what it was he rolled out of his truck?"

"Not really. It was big enough to be a person, but I didn't even try to get a good look. I was sort of freaked out. I just took off for home."

The sheriff studied the boy's face for a while longer, then

looked at the mom. "Thank you for coming in and telling us this."

What the hell? That was it—no more questions?

"You notice the color of the truck, Trevor?" Zak asked the question casually as if the answer wasn't that important.

Trevor's shoulders tensed. "Um, it was dark out."

"But there's a bright streetlamp right by the medical clinic. Can you remember if the truck drove through that light? Maybe you caught a glimpse?"

The boy turned to his mother who gave a slight nod. "You have to tell them, Trevor. Don't worry. As long as it's the truth you're doing the right thing."

"The truck was white with a green logo on the side. I couldn't read the words."

But Zak could tell by Trevor's guilty expression, that the boy knew what the words were, even though he hadn't seen them clearly. After all, Trevor had grown up in a community where the Sparks Construction logo was everywhere.

Zak checked the sheriff's expression, saw that his complexion had paled. He had to be drawing the obvious conclusion. Sparks Construction trucks had been designed to be distinctive—and there were no other vehicles in Lost Trail quite like them.

"Trevor was scared to tell you this," Patsy confided. "He was worried he might get his dad in trouble. Chris works for Sparks Construction, you know. But something like this— it's just too important to keep secrets."

"Yes, yes, you did the right thing by stepping forward, young man." The sheriff gazed off in the distance for a few seconds, then pulled in a breath and squared his shoulders. "The driver of the truck…would you say he was tall or short? Fat or thin?"

"He was a big, tall man, sir. Not really fat but—" Trevor held out his hands to indicate a big gut.

Zak felt suddenly both light-headed and elated. He'd been right.

Arranging for an illegal adoption, trying to "handle" the birth mother and eventually killing her—none of this stuff sounded like Derick. But it wasn't beyond the range of possibility for his father. Will Sparks was known for being a tough old bastard, a man used to getting what he wanted, and bulldozing over others to get it. In fact he was the only man in town Zak could remember his own father—also a tough old bastard—ever acting afraid of.

If Will Sparks *had* killed Riley and dumped her body out at the medical clinic, that would explain why Trevor had been afraid to say anything. Trevor's father worked for Sparks Construction. He wouldn't want to say something and risk his dad losing his job.

But now Trevor's description of the truck, where it had come from, and what the driver's physique had been like, could leave no doubt.

Yet the sheriff's expression didn't change an iota. "Okay. That's good to know. Thanks again, Trevor, Patsy." He offered his hand to each and then turned to Zak. "Take these fine folk to Butterfield. He can get Trevor's signed statement."

"Will do, Sheriff." As Zak led them out, Nadine brushed her way past him.

"Sheriff, can I have a word?"

She went in without closing the door behind her and as Zak pulled up chairs for Patsy and Trevor near Butterfield's desk, he overheard her talking.

"...the ex-boyfriend's name is Connor O'Leary. But he can't be the one who beat Riley to death. I just got off the phone with Detective Bowering. Connor O'Leary's been incarcerated under the California pimping and pandering laws for the past six months..."

At that point the door closed and Zak couldn't hear any more. Not that he needed to.

The sheriff's prime suspect was now in the clear and he'd been handed a clue for a new one. Question was...what would he do about it?

As soon as Trevor and Patsy left the office, the sheriff slipped on his shoulder holster and then grabbed his weathered sheepskin coat. "Going to pay Will and Jen Sparks a visit. Black, you're coming with me."

"Yes, Sheriff." Nadine snapped up at the order with a

let's go get 'em enthusiasm.

Butterfield half rose, looking like he was going to object, then abruptly sat back down and kept quiet. Zak wondered if he was remembering the large donation Sparks Construction always made to Sheriff Ford's election campaign. Maybe Butterfield was looking down the line to a time when he might be knocking on the Sparks's door looking for support?

Once they were gone, Zak made a show of keeping busy, but it was damn hard to concentrate. The price of being in the background meant that sometimes he had to wait to find out stuff. Normally he didn't mind, but today it was making him crazy. Once Trevor and Patsy were gone he made a show of needing to go down to the evidence lock-up in the basement, but once he was there, he dialed Tiff.

"All hell is breaking out here. I don't think you need to worry about Kenny anymore."

"What's happening?"

"I can't tell you now, but by this evening some of it might be public knowledge. Want to meet up at the Dew Drop later?"

"Sure. I'm assuming you don't think Kenny killed Riley."

"No. He looked like a top suspect for a while. But now…no. I'm almost positive he didn't kill Riley."

"That's a huge relief, but he still might be skimming money from our farm. I'm not sure how to tell Aunt Marsha and Mom. They think he walks on water."

"I'll help you map out a plan," he promised, though frankly fraud and theft did not seem nearly as important when there was a homicide about to be solved.

He was back at his desk for ten minutes at most when he heard footsteps climbing the stairs to the second floor. A moment later Aubrey Sparks walked in the door.

If it had been Elvis himself, back from the dead, Zak couldn't have been more surprised.

"Aubrey. You okay?"

She looked like she'd just gotten out of bed—hair uncombed, no makeup. Zak thought he could see pink flannel pajama bottoms peeking out between the hem of her full-length down coat and her suede Sorel boots.

"I just saw the sheriff drive up to my in-laws' house. He's in there talking to them right now and I...I need to talk to someone, too." Aubrey's voice betrayed a desperate nervousness. She glanced from Zak to Butterfield, then back again. "Zak, can I talk to you?"

Butterfield shrugged, a tacit signal to go ahead.

"Sure. Sit down. Can I get you a coffee?"

She shook her head to the offer of coffee, then perched on the chair and dug out some papers from her purse. One was a copy of the adoption agreement for Brody. The other was Brody's birth certificate. "Look at these. Do you see anything strange?"

He didn't at first. The adoption papers looked perfectly legal. The only detail that gave him pause was the name of the birth mother, which wasn't listed as Riley Concurran but a Miss Mary Peters. He felt the bitter crush of disappointment. His theory had seemed so clever, so perfect...and yet he must have been wrong. If Riley wasn't the mother of Will's grandson then what possible motive could there be for him to beat her to death?

He studied the birth certificate next and that was when he realized the point Aubrey was here to make. "You and Derick are listed as Brody's birth parents and yet you also have an adoption certificate for him." He looked to her for clarification.

"Exactly. You and I both know I'm not the mother, and I don't think Derick is the father either. Brody's real mother was coerced into impersonating me when she went to the hospital to give birth. I bet they paid her to do it. And to list Derick as the birth father."

A million questions sprang to mind at this wild theory. But almost immediately he saw the advantages to the Sparks family if they could convince—in other words pay—a pregnant woman to do what Aubrey suggested.

Without any record of being the birth mother, the woman would have no future claim to the child. No ability to rescind the adoption if she later changed her mind. And the child would have no way of ever seeking out his birth parents, either.

"But if that's true...what about these adoption papers?"

"They're fake, Zak. A little bit of make-believe Derick

and his parents came up with to make me believe I was legally adopting a baby boy—and not buying him from a woman they'd bribed to impersonate me when she went to the hospital to give birth."

Chapter Twenty-Eight

"I THOUGHT THIS was a legal adoption," Aubrey said. "But it was playacting. I believed I was in an adoption agency, but my in-laws rented an office and hired actors to fill the roles of lawyer and adoption agency manager."

Zak had no doubt she believed what she was saying. But it was such an audacious plan—were the Sparks capable of such deception?

"I know it seems insane. But it's true, Zak. I had this feeling everything was too good to be true…I mean it usually takes a long time to arrange an adoption, right? And ours came together in a matter of months."

If the Sparks had set up a fake adoption, they wouldn't have used the real birth mother's name on the papers—which meant his theory about Riley could still be correct. "When did you figure out the adoption was a sham?"

"At first it was a vague feeling I had that something was wrong. But then, about a month ago Derick and his parents started acting weird."

Which was when Riley Concurran moved to Lost Trail. The timing couldn't be a coincidence.

"Things got a lot worse once that poor woman was beaten to death. For the past ten days Derick has been impossible. He hasn't been sleeping and he snaps at everything I say. In all the five years we've been married I've never seen him act this way."

"Like he's under an unbearable amount of pressure." Not to mention guilt. "Is that why you have a bruise on your face? Did Derick hit you?"

She touched her cheek protectively. "No. Derick wouldn't. It was his father…"

He should have guessed. "When?"

"Derick and I were in the middle of a big argument one night when Will and Jen were coming to visit the baby. I made the mistake of saying something to them about their son being hard to get along with these days… Will went crazy. He slapped me. Hard. Then told me I was lucky to have a husband like Derick.

"That was when I first started to suspect Will and Jen were more involved than I'd thought. Then today when I saw the sheriff pull up at Derick's parents' house, and the sheriff and the deputy get out of the vehicle, I knew something was seriously wrong. I pushed Derick to tell me the truth, and it didn't take him long to confess. The guilt was practically choking him."

Zak was so engrossed in Aubrey's story, he was taken by surprise when the door burst open again. This time it was Derick holding his son swaddled in a thick, blue and yellow quilt.

Aubrey jumped from the chair, automatically holding out her arms for the baby. "I'm sorry, Derick. I've told Zak about the fake adoption."

The moment Derick relinquished the child his shoulders fell. "You did the right thing. This is all my fault. I never should have agreed to the plan. It sounded perfect when Dad and Mom explained it to me. But everything's gone horribly wrong."

Drawn in by the drama, Butterfield stepped forward and invited Aubrey and Derick to sit down. "Let's go through everything nice and calm, step by step. You'll feel better once it's all out in the open."

Zak didn't often agree with Butterfield, but in this case he thought the deputy was right. Derick was a straightforward guy, basically honest and kind. He wasn't built to handle guilt or to practice deception. The opportunity to confess was something he'd been yearning for, but it still couldn't be easy, not when it meant outing his parents.

"My mom and dad were only trying to help. They saw the stress Aubrey and I were under. They knew we'd been trying to have a child for almost five years."

"Why not be patient and adopt the regular way?"

"We've had some bad experiences with adoption in my family. I have a cousin who adopted a baby with her husband and then two months later the birth mother changed her mind and asked for the baby back. It broke my cousin's heart."

"And Will has a sister who adopted as well," Aubrey added. "When her son turned eighteen he pulled away from the family. Went to find his birth parents and ended up going to live near them to go to college. It tore the family apart."

"We didn't want to hurt anyone," Derick said. "Mom and Dad hired an investigator to find a pregnant woman who didn't want her baby and who wasn't in any shape to raise a child even if she did want one. They paid her well—I know that's illegal, but it didn't seem fair otherwise."

Zak could tell Butterfield wasn't connecting the dots, so he clarified, "And this birth mother—she was Riley Concurran, correct?"

Butterfield almost rolled off his chair as Derick and Aubrey nodded.

"And how did Riley find you?" Zak asked. "The whole point of this transaction was to have a perfectly clean-cut adoption, with no way for the birth mother to ever track down or claim the baby she'd given up."

"It was a stupid detail that gave us away," Derick said. "Dad gave Riley one of the company pens to sign the paperwork at the hospital. It had our company name, town, and state. Everything she needed to track us down."

"Why did she come?" Zak asked. "Had she changed her mind? Did she want the baby back?"

Derick let out a shaky sigh. "She claimed she wanted to make sure the baby had a good home. But once we showed her that he did, she still wasn't satisfied. She set up a meeting with Dad on Halloween night—"

"Do you know where they met?" Zak asked.

"The parking lot of Lost Creek Park. That's when she told him she wanted the baby back."

Butterfield's eyes were glistening. "At which point your dad lost his cool and hit her, right?"

Inwardly Zak groaned. Leading the witness much, Butterfield? "How did your dad react, Derick? Do you know?"

"I tried calling him that night. Neither him nor my mom answered. The next morning, when I heard Riley had been beaten—" he gulped "—to death, I went to see my dad. He refused to talk about it. He said, we were family, we'd stick together and get through this."

Derick's eyes were moist as he glanced from Butterfield to Zak. "But I can't believe my dad did it. And if he did swing out in anger, he sure didn't mean to kill her. Maybe there was someone else with them, some other guy who had a grudge against Riley."

Zak could understand why Derick would clutch at straws to defend his father. But Trevor had seen only one man dropping off something that might have been a body behind the medical clinic. And that man's truck and general size matched Will Sparks perfectly.

Chapter Twenty-Nine

WORK HAD ALWAYS provided a panacea for Justin when times were hard, so the morning after Willow left he threw himself into reviewing contracts. The day care drop-off had gone better than he'd expected. He was so grateful to Debbie-Ann for going out of her way to treat Geneva with kindness. She'd set up the little girl at the craft table with her daughter, Ashley, and the two little girls had been happily decorating pumpkin cut-outs when he left.

With his mind focused on other things, Justin didn't realize he'd worked through lunch until his father showed up in his office.

Clark Pittman eased his frame into one of the two upholstered chairs that were positioned in front of Justin's desk. "I looked for you at the Snowdrift. Not taking lunch today?"

Justin glanced at the time display on his computer. "Wow, the morning flew by. Want to grab a sandwich now?"

"I'd like to, Son, but I'm headed to Missoula. The medical examiner is performing the autopsy on Riley Concurran's body today and I plan to sit in. Did you hear the sheriff made an arrest this morning?"

Justin dropped his pen. "He did? Who?"

"You're not going to believe this—Will Sparks."

One of Justin's major clients was Sparks Construction. Before Derick took over management of the company, he'd had business meetings with Will practically every month. Will was tough with a quick temper, but he was also a devoted family man. Justin couldn't imagine him messing around with a young woman like Riley. "That's insane. Has our sheriff turned into a loose cannon?"

Neither he nor his father had a high opinion of Archie Ford's intellectual abilities. But Ford was a good man for keeping law and order, and generally the people of Bitterroot County respected him for that.

"It's a complicated story, but here's the bare-bones theory. Riley Concurran is the birth mother of Will's new grandson."

"What?"

"Allegedly Will Sparks hired an investigator to find a pregnant woman who would be willing to sell them her baby. They wanted someone young and desperate, someone from a major city far from Montana with no family or support system. The investigator came up with Riley."

"Good God." This sort of thing was illegal but it probably happened more often than most people would think. Families with money and power—even if they were just big fish in a small pond like the Sparks family—often didn't think the "rules" applied to them.

"I never told you this, Dad, but Riley came to my office once asking if an attorney had to turn in a client if he knew they'd done something illegal. I wondered what crime she was speaking of. Honestly, I suspected drugs. But it must have been this—she'd sold her baby."

"Yes. The Sparks thought they'd covered all their tracks but their plan went sideways when Riley showed up in Lost Trail, allegedly this time wanting the baby back. The theory goes that when she made her demands at a clandestine meeting on Halloween night Will lost his temper. Big time."

"Will the sheriff be able to prove any of this?"

"Most of the evidence is circumstantial. But an eyewitness saw a Sparks Construction truck drive out from Lost Creek Road around three a.m. on Halloween night. A man fitting Will's general description was alone in the truck. He carried something large out of his truck—about the size of a human body—and then drove off."

Justin whistled. "Was this witness close enough to see his face?"

"No, but there's more. This morning Aubrey and Derick confessed to the illegal so-called adoption. According to Aubrey, Will Sparks arranged the entire thing."

"I can almost see Will and perhaps Jen, too, coming up with a plan like this. But why would Derick and Aubrey go along with it?" They were such a nice couple, and Derick was reasonably intelligent with a humble and kind manner about him, quite the opposite of his father's.

"Aubrey was kept in the dark. She thought the adoption was legal and above board—until Derick started falling apart under the guilt and she convinced him to tell her the truth. As for Derick, he was under a lot of pressure from his wife who was desperate to be a mom, and his parents who wanted a grandchild and heir for the family business."

"Man. This is one messed-up town, Dad." Justin retrieved his pen and spun it around with one hand—a trick Paul had taught him during their first-year economics course. "I'm afraid I've got news of my own, and it isn't good."

Clark's eyes widened with alarm. "Are Willow and Geneva okay?"

Justin leaned back in his chair. "Geneva's fine. But Willow's gone."

As was his way, his father took some time to think over the statement before replying calmly, "You mean she's left you?"

Justin nodded. "She left Geneva too. In hindsight I suspect Willow came back to Lost Trail for exactly this purpose. To set me up as Geneva's legal guardian, so she could go back to Paul."

Clark made an expression of distaste. This development would only confirm his low opinion of Willow.

"You told me Paul is Geneva's biological father. I take it he never wanted the child?"

"Having a child cramped Paul's lifestyle too much. It's

just a hunch on my part, but I'm guessing he may have become abusive toward her and that's why Willow came to me. She knew I wouldn't turn her away. My guess is Willow is hoping she and Paul can go back to their old globe-trotting, pleasure-seeking days now that they don't have a little kid complicating their lives."

His father gave a tired sigh. "I'm sorry, Son. You deserve so much better."

"Don't worry about me." Oddly enough, though a corner of his heart was broken, Justin didn't have it in him to be angry with Willow. He knew too well the pull of Paul's magnetic personality. "It's Geneva I'm concerned about."

"That poor child. How is she doing?"

"She's pretty sad. They say kids are resilient though. Maybe she'll be okay here with us?"

"Kids are tougher than they look. You handled your mother's death much better than I did. Together we muddled through."

"We did better than muddle. I lucked out when it came to fathers, Dad."

"Geneva's lucked out too, though she may not realize it yet."

"THERE ARE PEOPLE in this world who think their money should buy them anything," Kenny said. "I guess Will Sparks is one of them."

Tiff nodded. She'd just gotten off the phone with Zak when the farm manager had sauntered into her office. She'd filled Kenny in on the arrest and the apparent motive behind the homicide. "I'm not sure what will happen to the baby, but Will's going to be doing jail time, Zak is pretty sure, even if his attorney convinces the court Will never intended to kill Riley. All the Sparks family's money won't get Will out of that."

"Speaking of money..." Kenny leaned forward in his chair. "I'm guessing you've figured out the balance in the books for investments doesn't match the balance in the bank?"

Tiff hadn't expected Kenny to raise the subject. She gathered the pages strewn around her desk together and tapped them into a neat bundle. "I figured that out the first day I started working here. If you knew there was a problem, why didn't you tell me?"

Kenny rubbed the one-day growth on his jaw. "I should have. But I was freaking out. When I was in high school my dad, who worked as an investment advisor, was investigated for fraud. After years of court cases he ended up in prison for cheating several clients out of hundreds of thousands of dollars. My mom stuck by him right through the whole thing, but I was so ashamed. Still am. My dad had been my hero, you know? And then to find out he'd done something like that, well, I haven't had much to do with either of them since I left home."

Tiff didn't know what to say. Any kid would feel betrayed in a situation like that. But he still hadn't explained why he hadn't told her the truth.

"Bookkeeping isn't my strong suit," Kenny continued. "It wasn't until a few days before you came home that I realized we had a problem with the accounts. I got scared, and, I'll admit it, a little irrational too. I figured you'd find out about my dad and just assume I'd taken the money. I wanted to find the mistake in the accounts first, so I could prove I was innocent."

"Is that what you were doing in the office late on Tuesday night?"

"You knew I was here?"

"Couldn't sleep, so I was wandering. My brother's bedroom has a perfect view of both your cabin and the office."

"Guilty as charged. I grabbed the bank statements so I could study them at night and try to find the problem. I figured if I could prove money had started going missing before I was hired, I'd be in the clear." He rubbed his hands on his thighs, as if trying to rid himself of an unseen stain. "But I put in hours and still couldn't figure it out. Today I decided there was nothing left to do but come clean. So here's the truth, Tiff. The money's missing but I swear to God I didn't take it."

"I believe you."

"You do?"

"The bank got me access to the older records today and I was able to trace the missing money back to well before you started working here. It looks like Ed had been siphoning off one or two hundred dollars every month since my father died and he took over. After twenty years, the figures started adding up."

"You're sure it was Ed doing the skimming?"

"Yes. The discrepancy between the accounts and the investment account was getting so large, he must have been afraid he was about to get caught. And so he quit."

"The bastard."

"No kidding. This is going to kill my mom and aunt. They trusted Ed implicitly. If he'd asked for a raise, they would have given it to him. But to find out he was stealing from them…" She left her papers and went to sit beside Kenny on the sofa.

"I'm sorry for your family. But I'm incredibly relieved you've cleared me of any wrongdoing. I like it here, Tiff."

"Don't be angry, but for a while, I wondered if you and Riley had been having an affair—if maybe you'd gone into town to meet up with her that night she was killed."

"That damned piece of pink underwear… I didn't want to say anything—it felt ungallant—but Riley did come on to me that night she was killed. All the other workers had gone and she'd stayed behind to take a shower. I was grappling with paperwork, figured she'd drive off when she was done like she usually did."

"But she didn't?"

"She comes in here, totally naked, carrying those panties in her hand. Goes straight to the sofa and asks if I'd like to join her."

"And you…?" Was he tempted? From all accounts Riley had been a pretty woman.

"I told her if she valued her job to cut that shit out. And no messing around with the crew either. She backtracked fast. Said she was trying to show me she was grateful for the job. I told her I didn't work that way."

"She sounded pretty messed up."

"She was used to dealing with people who expected her to give them something for everything she got. She figured I'd given her a job and I would expect payback. It's pretty damn sad."

"Or maybe she was seeking a distraction. She must have been nervous about the meeting she'd set up with Will Sparks later that night."

Kenny nodded slowly. "Yeah, that could be it."

Tiff had been watching him closely as he talked, realizing with some surprise that not only did she believe his explanation for not coming clean about the missing money, she also didn't find him nearly as obnoxious as she once had. "It is sad. Riley was so young…she had lots of time to turn her life around."

"I'm glad your mother and aunt are going to give her a proper burial."

Tiff nodded. "Then maybe we can put this behind us…and you and I can have a fresh start. I'm sorry I've been acting like a spoiled brat."

"I wouldn't go that far. You're protective of the farm and your family. That's a good thing. I'm glad you've figured out I'm not such a bad guy, though."

"Maybe we could have another Dark and Stormy one night."

"I have a feeling it's going to be a long winter. Maybe we'll have more than one."

✕

Tiff had a pitcher of draft beer on the table when Zak made it to the Dew Drop shortly after six that evening. The place was already busy with local ranchers and townspeople celebrating the end of the work week. And it would get a lot more crowded shortly.

Zak walked in sporting a big grin and sat with a sigh of satisfaction. "Thanks for saving a table."

"You bet. I've been dying to talk to you. Mom and Aunt Marsha are still in shock—neither one can believe Will Sparks would do something like this."

"I don't believe he meant to kill Riley. But he's a strong man with a bad temper. We've arrested the right man, I have no doubt about that."

"I agree." Nadine, approaching their table, had obviously

overheard his last remark.

Zak had seen her enter the bar, and had watched as she scanned the room, checking his natural impulse to wave her over. He still wasn't sure where he stood with her. The hectic pace at the office today had afforded them zero time to talk.

"Hey, Nadine, I hear you've had a busy day," Tiff said.

"It was pretty crazy," Nadine agreed.

"Want to join us for a beer?" Zak asked.

After the briefest of pauses she shrugged and said, "Sure."

Zak signaled Mari to bring another glass. "Tiff was just telling me how shocked her family is about Will Sparks's arrest."

"I'm new to the community," Nadine said. "But from what I've seen the guy strikes me as the type used to getting what he wants and willing to bend the rules if it's of benefit to him."

"Good assessment," Tiff said. "I just feel so awful for Derick. His parents no doubt bullied him into this plan. Do you think he'll be charged, too?"

"I doubt it, especially if he agrees to testify against his dad." Nadine thanked Mari as the server filled a new glass with some lager from the pitcher.

The three of them raised their glasses.

"Here's to—" Tiff drew a blank. "I'm not sure what to drink to on a day like this."

"Survival?" Nadine suggested.

Zak grinned. "We made it through the day. Yeah, here's

to survival."

"I could use a change of subject," Tiff said, turning to Nadine. "When I was a little girl I dreamed about being in the rodeo one day. I'd love to hear what it was like to be a champion barrel racer."

"Periods of great excitement and adrenaline rushes followed by long stretches of hard work, travel, boredom, and loneliness."

"That's quite the nutshell. I've watched some of your races on YouTube. You and your horse had an amazing connection."

Sadness seeped over Nadine's face. "Mane Event is the only thing I miss about those days."

"I'm sorry." Tiff put her hand briefly over Nadine's.

"More than anything I wish Mane Event could have lived to enjoy the retirement she'd earned. But getting a job in law enforcement—I think it was a smart move for me. It's been an adjustment in a lot of ways. But I like the work. Even this pokey town is growing on me."

"I hated the remoteness when I was a teenager. But Lost Trail has its charms. The scenery for one. Old friends for another." Tiff smiled at Zak.

He returned the smile. He hadn't realized how much he'd missed his old friend until she'd moved back. "This town needs people like you."

"Thanks, Zak."

Mari came around then, and they ordered another pitcher of draft as well as burgers and fries.

"Hey, my farm manager Kenny Bombard just came in." Tiff got up from the table. "Mind if I ask him to join us?"

"Go right ahead." Zak watched as she went to greet the tall guy standing near the entrance, weighing his options in the crowded room. With his messy dark hair and scruff of a beard, he looked a little rough for Tiff. But who knew?

"Hot guy," Nadine commented, confirming his total lack of understanding about what women wanted in men. "You jealous?"

Zak shook his head wearily. "You still gnawing on that old bone?"

She laughed. "Maybe it's time to let it go. You're a lot more complicated than I thought, Zak Waller. I can't figure you out."

"I'm just a simple guy, living a simple life, in a simple town."

"Hah! I might have believed that about you at one time. But no more." Her gaze turned probing. "You totally solved this case, Zak."

The admiring look she gave him made him uncomfortable.

"And yet you're not taking any of the credit."

"Drop it, would you? I'm not looking for credit."

"That's the part I can't figure out."

He shrugged. "It's not complicated. I like my life the way it is." That was no longer totally true. But until he figured out what he *did* want, it would be his official position.

"I'm not sure I believe you. But one thing's going to change going forward."

"Oh?"

"I won't underestimate you a second time."

They fell silent as Mari came to deliver their burgers. From the other side of the room Tiff and Kenny began to make their way to their table.

"Thanks, Mari." Zak lifted the top off his burger. Yup, onions. He began picking them off.

"Going for your usual run Sunday morning?" Nadine asked, reaching past him for the catsup.

"Of course. Want to join me?"

"Count on it."

Zak paused to study her face. The look she gave him was intriguing. It wasn't just his career he needed to rethink. He might also have to revisit his no romance at work policy.

Epilogue

O N THE MORNING of Riley Concurran's graveside service, the sun was shining, the Montana sky was a brilliant blue, and Tiff was grateful even the weather was paying its proper respects. Riley's school-girl friend, Emily Blake, had flown to Missoula from San Francisco last night. Kenny and Tiff had picked her up at the airport and taken her to Raven Farm. Over the dinner table last night Emily's stories of Riley's past had given Tiff, her aunt and mother, and Kenny some laughs. They'd also shared a fair number of tears.

Now the five of them stood at the graveside, Tiff between her mother and her aunt, with Kenny and Emily right behind them. While the priest spoke of redemption, eternal love, and peace, Tiff thought about Riley's life. Thanks to Emily she knew it hadn't all been hard. But it was sobering to realize how a few bad knocks could send a good person reeling. The death of Riley's mother had started the downward spiral, proving how important family and a sense of community were to a person.

Despite her losses—and Tiff was very aware of the two

gravestones several rows behind her—Tiff felt lucky to still have her mother and her aunt, her friends, and of course the land and the farm.

She glanced at Aubrey, standing on the other side of the open grave, dressed in black, and holding Brody like he was the most precious treasure in the world. Riley's life had ended tragically, but at least she'd left behind a legacy—her adorable son.

After some consideration Family Services had decided to leave the little boy in Aubrey's custody. If there had been any other biological family alive it might have worked out differently, but since Aubrey had been totally innocent of the Sparks family's scheming, she'd been judged the best person to care for Brody.

She and Derick were currently separated, and though he stood well apart from his wife and child, Derick's eyes, moist with tears, were on them now. His mother stood beside him, shrouded in a black hat and veil. To what extent Jen had played a part in the adoption scheme and Riley's death, no one knew for sure, though Zak had told Tiff he suspected Derick and Will had made a pact to protect Jen at all costs.

Justin Pittman was also at the funeral, standing beside his father. The two were so different physically, but emotionally they were tight, even more so now that Willow had left Justin in the lurch. Geneva wasn't at the funeral, but at church last week Sybil had told Tiff the little girl was adjusting well to her new father and living circumstances. All the more credit to Justin.

The service was almost over when Tiff finally spotted Zak. He was standing near the back of the small assemblage. Of course he was. With his hand pressed to his chest, he was listening intently to the service. Or was he? Suddenly he caught her eye and winked.

Though Zak's name hadn't been mentioned in any of the broadcasts or news articles about the resolution of the case, Tiff—among a handful of others—knew he'd been instrumental in solving it. Zak was so good at being humble, even she, one of his best friends, hadn't realized how smart he was.

But she knew now. And she was suddenly filled with a sense of optimism about the future. She no longer looked at her move home a last desperate option—it had also been her best. She was looking forward to growing her business, helping her mother…and possibly enjoying a new romance.

Lost Trail might be a dying town, but it wasn't a lost cause yet. A new generation was getting ready to take the reins. She was going to be part of that movement. And so—even if he didn't know it yet—was Zak.

The End

Bitter Root Mystery Series

On the surface Lost Trail, Montana is a picture-perfect western town offering beautiful mountain scenery and a simple way of life revolving around the local ranches as well as a nearby ski resort. But thirty-year old Tiff Masterson and her former school-chum Zak Waller—dispatcher at the local Sheriff's office—know there is darkness in this town, too, an evil with roots that neither of them fully understand.

Book 1: *Bitter Roots*

Book 2: *Bitter Truth*

Book 3: *Bitter Sweet*

About the Author

USA Today Bestselling author C. J. Carmichael has written over 50 novels with more than three million copies in print. She has been nominated for the *RT Bookclub's* Career Achievement in Romantic Suspense award, and is a three time nominee for the *Romance Writers of America* RITA Award.

Visit C.J.'s website at CJCarmichael.com

Thank you for reading

Bitter Roots

If you enjoyed this book, you can find more from all our great authors at TulePublishing.com, or from your favorite online retailer.

TULE
PUBLISHING

Printed in Great Britain
by Amazon